The Light in the Sound

a novel

V. G. Anderson

BREAD & BEAUTY PRESS

BREAD & BEAUTY PRESS

1037 NE 65th St
Ste #80814
Seattle, WA 98115

info@breadandbeautypress.com
www.breadandbeautypress.com

Cover design by NightOwlFreelance.com
Cover art © Claudia Lucia McKinney at PhatPuppyArt.com

Manufactured in the United States of America

Second edition October 2018

Hardback ISBN-13: 978-1-949193-97-8
Paperback ISBN-13: 978-0-9990126-6-6

Further praise for *The Light in the Sound*

"V. G. Anderson's debut novel, *The Light in the Sound*, is unusually smart, containing as it does characters and insights that give us a cool and often funny look into the Millennial generation. But the story is also realistic and compelling, showing the struggle of a generation trying to find its way in a world in which our traditional national assumptions were abandoned, leaving these wonderful young people flying blind."

—Philip F. Deaver, Flannery O'Connor award-winning author of *Silent Retreats* and *Forty Martyrs*

"A spirited debut novel by the exuberant new voice of V. G. Anderson, *The Light in the Sound* takes you into the zany, sometimes dark world of streets and bars where good kids get away from bad families and grow themselves into people worth knowing. At the heart of this novel is smart, spunky Rachel Richardson, once a high school runaway, now 24, employed in an adult store selling edible underwear and snacking on penis chocolates while trying to figure out a better future for herself. Maybe this future will include her old crush Justin from her hometown working in a nearby camera shop or maybe the gorgeous, intuitive, crazy girl Cerise, but for sure it will include the truth and imagination and morality that were absent from her broken, hypocritical Mormon home. Despite panic and wee hour visions, Rachel is one plucky character, honest and winsome and playful and funny, grounded, loveable, a bit wacky, courageous, insightful, and aware. It is sheer delight to take this coming of age journey with her."

–Julie Brickman, author of *What Birds Can Only Whisper* and *Two Deserts*

"In a dysfunctional world, V. G. Anderson deftly weaves together religion, family, relationships, and love through the eyes of Rachel, a disaffected young woman working in a porn store, who is left with a better—but fragile—understanding of her world. With humor and pathos, Anderson creates genuinely sympathetic characters whom we have all met and surely recognize."

—TJ Rivard, published stories *Café Irreal, Flashquake, SmokeLong Quarterly, Gulf Stream Magazine*, and Pushcart Prize nominee

"From the very first sentence of *The Light in the Sound* by V. G. Anderson, the reader wants to know the story of Rachel, a young woman with a troubled past. A thought-provoking coming of age story, this book explores the full range of relationships: boyfriends, girlfriends, and ultimately family. Through it all, Rachel is brave and full of hope. She not only wins our sympathy but our admiration."

—Karen Mann, author of *The Woman of La Mancha* and *The Saved Man*

For Josh & Jubilee

"Try to be a rainbow in someone's cloud."

—Maya Angelou, *Letter to my Daughter*

The Light in the Sound

Guide to Salvation

Rachel is having trouble sleeping and searches the kitchen for edible consolation. Her birthday was a few days ago. She had purchased a small, round, yellow cake with purple, buttercream frosting; the remaining half mocks her endless battle to button her favorite jeans. Weighing a few moments of oral pleasure against hours of guilt for eating something indulgent has always been a struggle, but bad nights are becoming too frequent to rationalize a 4:00 a.m. binge session.

Having left her parents' home at age sixteen, she has lived alone for eight years now, yet still struggles to sleep. Attaching a small chain on the front door helped. It's been a while since she woke up lying in the grass outside her apartment or on a neighbor's couch. She has no control over what her grade-school counselor referred to as night-terrors, which Rachel prefers to call *middle-dreams* because her mind is trapped somewhere between wake and sleep in a place so much closer to awake that she might as well be.

Besides the immediate emotional trauma that she can usually shrug off by lunch, most of her sleep disturbances are harmless, laughable even. But tonight, she had pinched her thumb in the bedroom door while frantically trying to escape a shadowy figure she thought was climbing through the window. The result is a throbbing blood-blister distracting her from the contents of the refrigerator. Glancing at the small clock on the kitchen wall, she groans.

Next to the couch she had purchased at a thrift store and covered with a red-chenille throw, are stacks of books and magazines. At the top of the stack is a fashion mag. Page 57 had inspired Rachel's long, layered haircut and burgundy-brown dye that apparently complements her pink skin tone. But she doesn't feel like it looks as good on her as it does on the blemish-free model. She wonders if the model was smiling in the original photo or if they airbrushed that as well.

Rachel's mother, Emily, used to send music and magazines from all over the world. But her stepmother is devoutly religious and believes that magazines represent one of the evils that entrap people to live *of the world* instead of just in it. To Rachel, they offered tutorials on shades of eyeshadow to accentuate her hazel eyes. She also enjoyed reading the stories, and doing the silly quizzes, then hid them under the bed with her makeup, so her stepmother wouldn't scold. Now fashion magazines just make her feel overweight and poor. She grabs it and marches back into the kitchen. Tossing it atop the full trash, the magazine falls to the floor. She considers salvaging the unused perfume sample, then kicks the crumpled pages closer to the can and walks away.

Her fat, short-legged, calico cat, Ewoka, is stretched out on the couch. Rachel scoots her out of the way to retrieve the television remote. Banging it against her palm, the dying batteries finally work, and the television buzzes to life. Infomercials selling false hope fill most channels. A beautiful actor in a long, white, billowy skirt holding a bright-green bottle of shampoo, smiles while twirling in a lemon-colored room. The girl whips a silky head of blonde hair in an unnatural motion. Rachel sighs while pressing the red button until the room falls silent. Drowsiness is overwhelming. Sun peeks through cracks in the living room blinds, and the rumble of a cracked muffler fades into the distance. Comforted by the waking world, she considers going back to bed, but music playing on the alarm clock in the bedroom reminds her that she's out of time for sleep.

She strips in front of the long bathroom mirror and scrutinizes her body. She's thin, but she never feels thin enough. Lately, her body image is worse because she had recently gained a few pounds and can see every last one clinging to her hips, inner thighs, and disappearing waistline. As if each place had gained all of it. Fortunately, her breasts are also plumper, and only moderately uneven—not noticeable when dressed. Unlike Sadie, her best friend, who stitches together the cups from padded and regular bras to create what she refers to as the "super bra" for symmetry.

Scowling at the deep lines slowly appearing beneath her eyes, Rachel wonders what she'll look like by age forty. Relaxing into normal posture, she makes a fart-like noise to serenade her frump, and then carefully steps into the shower.

The Light in the Sound

The warm water and citrus shampoo bubbles are soothing. She imagines herself as the girl in the commercial and poses for the seashell designs on the shower curtain, as if hidden cameras inside each image are capturing her exaggerated movements. She lathers her hair, smiling for the imaginary audience, then chokes on soapy water. Thinking she hears her cell-phone ring, she pauses. Nothing. She picks up the pace not to be late for work. Tiptoeing down the hallway in search of the towel she forgot—still folded on the kitchen table—creates a trail of soggy carpet, and beads of cool water prickle her skin. This spring is even colder than normal for Seattle, but this morning is one of the worst in weeks. She wants to move somewhere warm, like a tropical beach. She thinks people always look happy strolling down the beach, nothing like the stern faces atop business suits racing down a city street. She puts on her favorite pair of faded jeans, a blue fleece hooded sweatshirt, and black Converse shoes, checks her cellphone for missed calls, and grabs her keys.

Defrosting ice on the windshield of her silver, '68 Dodge Charger takes forever. She hates waiting for it to warm up, but she loves her car. It has only thirty-thousand original miles and runs great. A few years ago, Emily showed up unexpectedly (her M.O.) and offered to sell the car to Rachel who was desperately in need of a vehicle. Emily was on her way back to South America with a new boyfriend and needed to dump the car fast, so the deal was mutually beneficial. They had agreed on a few-thousand dollars that Rachel could pay in installments, but Emily had disappeared without leaving a contact number or address—just the keys, title, and a note that said, "Once she hits ¼ tank you've got five minutes to find a gas station." Rachel assumes Emily will eventually be back to collect. In the meantime, Rachel's grateful for the car, which has more character than her friends' little fiberglass death traps—and guys love it.

Freezing air turns foggy as she blows warm breath into her cupped hands. She thumbs through CDs for something to keep her awake on the way to work and inserts a mix. Kenny Loggins, *Footloose*, blares out of the speakers. She adjusts the rearview to check for missed eyeliner globs—rubs one off, then licks her finger and runs it over a section of hair thinking for itself.

Justin—a new friend with boyfriend potential—works today, and she doesn't want to look like she's trying too hard. It's bad enough that after not seeing him for ten years (since having a crush on him in junior high) she wound up working in the porn shop next to the camera store where he works. Despite his seemingly non-judgmental attitude, she doesn't want to look, or act, like a girl who works in the sex industry. She fears a dating life that mirrors her stripper friends, consisting of nothing but emotional abandonment in the wake of a long string of one-night stands.

Rachel pulls into the parking lot of the strip-mall where she's worked for the past two years. Rain-soaked, cedar shingles bulge on the side of the building. Only a few shop owners have put out their sandwich-board signs because the previous night's storm left ankle-deep puddles of water in the uneven sidewalk. Watching the clock, she counts down her last minute, shoves a stick of spearmint gum into her mouth, and heads for the entrance to the small shop where she'll be trapped for the next eight hours. Pink bells hanging from the door handle announce her arrival. The new girl—whose name Rachel forgot—runs out from the back room to greet her.

"It's you," new girl says with exaggerated relief. "I thought you were gonna be late. I was about to call you."

Rachel nods, says, "Hey," and rushes to the back room, shutting the door behind her. She clocks-in, then carefully slips the mandatory store-alarm necklace under her shirt. She's doesn't want to be the punchline of next week's jokes—the most recent idiot to lose her commission by accidentally pressing the button and filling the parking lot with police cars that scare away customers. After hiding in the bathroom as long as she can, she heads out to the sales floor to begin her day. "You're way overdressed for casual Friday," she says.

New girl hops off the stool behind the checkout counter, throws her shoulders back, and says, "This is an upscale lingerie store, and I want to represent it accordingly."

"This isn't a classy shop. This is a porn shop. Even if they change the fuchsia walls to solid gold, high priced lingerie will never mask the fact that we sell sex, not clothes."

New girl's shoulders drop.

"All I'm saying is this ain't *Victoria's Secret*, and even then. You don't have to do the song and dance for me. If I could come to work in my pajamas, I would. I doubt the people we deal with all week would care. Hell, they'd probably like it... Don't get me started on how many orgy-invites I've had."

New girl slumps forward; her eyes get glossy.

Rachel hates the jargon they feed everyone in orientation about female *empowerment* and embracing your sexuality. She had heard the *helping-couples-in-need* speech. But after battery testing god-only-knows how many vibrators and giving people the non-returnable disclaimer so many times she can do it in her sleep, all the empowerment they blew up her ass had lost its luster. "Trust me, accept it for what it is and you'll last a lot longer here."

"What is it?"

"A shitty job that pays ten times better than McDonald's."

"Well, I find it liberating."

"So what area of the store do you want to stock today while you're being *liberated?* There's a stack of magazines in the back displaying the amazing feats of a nine-inch schlong. Or would you rather stock the new DVDs featuring what *has* to be Oscar worthy performances of midgets—excuse me, little people—blowing their wads on each other's faces? I assume the DVDs because they're near the *classy* corsets that come with a matching ball-gag."

New girl scowls, balls up her fists, and locks her elbows, mumbling as she stomps away.

The bells on the door jingle and a young man wearing a white polo shirt with a floral shop logo walks in. He's holding two dozen pink roses—almost the same shade as his cheeks after he nearly collides with a display of edible underwear and flavored condoms. Rachel thinks he's cute.

He sets the bundle on the counter. A happy birthday card attached to a clear stem stands above most of the flowers. "I have a delivery for Rachel Richardson," he says.

"Who from?" she asks—hoping he'll say Justin. She squeezes the edge of the counter so tight her knuckles turn bright white.

He digs a crumpled yellow piece of paper out of his pocket

with a couple coins and a ball of fuzz. "Chuck Halsted," he finally says.

Every hopeful butterfly in her stomach abruptly dies, creating a pileup that feels like a lead weight in her gut. Rachel had hung out with Chuck a few times but blocked his number after discovering he lied about being single. His wife saw a couple of Rachel's flirtatious texts, then called—accusing her of being a home-wrecker, yelling about their four children until Rachel finally hung up. She had no idea, but she still felt awful.

"Can I refuse them?" she asks.

He looks more flustered than when he first noticed the small, foil wrapped penis-shaped chocolates in the basket by the cash register. "That doesn't happen very often, but, yeah."

"Sorry—I'm gonna have to, but thanks for the trouble."

He nods and turns to leave, staring straight ahead, like a gymnast on a balance beam.

Worried that Charles is lurking somewhere in the parking lot, she hides behind the front window display that had earned her accolades from management last week. Two mannequins with bright-blue Cleopatra wigs, scantily clad in black and yellow lingerie are standing next to each other facing the window. The hand of one grasps the end of a chain connected to a black-leather studded choker around the neck of the other mannequin holding a short flicker whip.

New girl stands beside Rachel.

"So, what do people call you—do you have a nickname?" Rachel asks, trying to hide that she still doesn't remember her name.

"Nah, everybody just calls me Neeka."

Two gay guys, three couples, an eager boy who looks so young Neeka asks to see his ID, then tells to leave, and a girl in her late-twenties stocking up for a bachelorette party, burn the morning. Finally, Justin's truck pulls into the parking lot. Rachel snaps out of her midday trance to check her hair and makeup. She tries not to stare as he opens the door of his new, blue, ½-ton pickup truck, and lets his leg dangle for a moment before hopping out and setting the alarm.

He glances in the direction of the porn shop, but doesn't seem to look past the window display, then disappears into the shop next door.

"...over there. What do you think?" Neeka asks.

"Sorry—what?"

"I think we should move the edible underwear over there." Neeka points to a corner of the shop with nothing but a pale mannequin wearing black-glitter star pasties and crotchless panties. "It seems like a lot of people are running into the edible underwear display. I think we need to clear a wider path for people, so they aren't so overwhelmed when they walk in."

Neeka reminds Rachel of an Anime character in a Hentai film. She imagines her short black hair tied up in pigtails with purple ribbons, and an overweight white man with a cigar hanging out of his mouth grunting as he bends her over and lifts her plaid skirt—

Neeka squints at Rachel.

"Yeah, sure, whatever—I'm gonna go get something to wake me up—be back in a minute," Rachel says.

She walks to the end of the strip-mall for a smoothie, and a glimpse of Justin. Hopefully. Cars on the busy street splash through pools of water. The air is thick with auto exhaust. Bright sun reflecting off a windshield makes her temples throb. Loud clangs and bangs coming from the tire shop at the end of the complex echo through the parking lot. She's careful not to glance in the camera store as she walks by. The plan is to stop in and say hello as she heads back to work, so she'll have an excuse not to stay too long and seem overly interested, but she hopes he'll notice her.

She enters the bright, pastel pink and orange smoothie bar that had opened a week ago and appreciates the invigorating scent of mixed berries. A woman wearing blue leggings that are three sizes too small is blocking the order line. Rachel gawks as the woman steps aside to wait for her order.

"I'm gonna need a minute," she says to a blonde-haired girl in a lime-green visor, glancing back to make sure no one else is waiting in line.

The blonde turns around and shouts a request for more shaved ice to a lurpy guy in the back hovered over a blender filled with fuchsia goo.

The door beeps. A line is growing behind her.

"I'll have a Pineapple-Orange Twister," she says quickly, frustrated for having only glanced over half the menu.

"Make that two," Justin says, smiling, as he slips past Rachel, laying a twenty-dollar bill on the counter.

The cashier takes the money and smirks.

"You don't have to do that," Rachel says.

"I owe you for the donuts last week."

She pauses—not sure how to avoid letting him pay

without making the situation more awkward.

"Seriously, we're good. Just let me get this." He moves off to the side, making way for the customer she hadn't heard come in. She also notices the woman in the blue leggings is gone. She feels disoriented. Justin motions for her to sit by him at a round yellow table in the corner.

"Since you paid for my drink, I suppose I have to sit with you," she teases.

"You could always sit by *lover boy*." Justin points to the employee she had noticed earlier—now sitting in the opposite corner, conspicuously picking his nose while reading a comic book.

Rachel grimaces. "Let's hope they have a strict hand-washing policy."

Justin laughs.

"Thanks, by the way." Rachel smiles, enjoying the prolonged eye contact. Enough for her to hope that paying for the smoothie was more than just a *friendly* gesture.

Justin is tall with wide shoulders, an olive complexion, light-brown hair, and an understated sense of humor. He always seems laid-back and confidently self-aware. All of which, Rachel finds attractive. But seeing him hunched over, twirling a straw—obviously vulnerable to her smile, makes her want to lean across the table and kiss him. Instead, she flicks a wadded straw wrapper at his head, then stands up to get their drinks.

"So how do you like working at the porn shop?" he asks as she sits back down. "It doesn't seem like *you*."

She assumes he's referring to first meeting her back when she was still attending Sunday-school. She shoves the straw in her mouth and takes a prolonged swig to avoid answering. As compelled as she is to tell him every detail of her life, she thinks better of it. But she's alarmed by how comfortable he makes her feel. Like if she tells him everything, he might actually listen. She gets the sense that he might even *want* to listen. But she's not the type to dump her life story on everyone who makes eye contact or buys her a smoothie, so she keeps her answer simple, "It's cool."

"I developed your film last night. You can come pick it up any time," he says between gulps. "No offense, but you take some pretty weird pictures."

Rachel smiles. "I'll explain it after I see them."

Justin glances at his watch and stands up to leave. "How 'bout I bring them over on my break, so I have time for this mysterious explanation."

"Sounds good." She follows him out and barely avoids running into a trashcan while staring at his ass. Somehow, she finds her way safely back to the porn shop just in time to overhear an old man with slurred speech demand Neeka's phone number. Rachel slips behind the counter and stares at the violet shopping bag in the man's hand. "I see you've completed your purchase. Is there anything else I can help you find today, sir?"

He looks startled that she seemingly appeared out of nowhere. "Uh…no, I just—" He groans and heads for the door. A cloud of stale cigarette, and the sour scent of box-wine follow him out.

The bells hanging on the door slam hard against the glass.

"Creepy," Rachel says.

Neeka sighs. She buttons her low-cut blouse one higher

and rubs the chain of her alarm necklace. Her tiny hand is shaking.

"Sorry I took so long."

Neeka grins. "I saw Justin run out after you left."

Rachel slurps the end of one of the best smoothies she's ever had. "Hey—you should take your break."

Neeka puts on her black peacoat to leave and buttons it unevenly.

I give her two weeks, Rachel thinks.

While Neeka is gone, Rachel wanders around the store playing with a pair of fuzzy purple handcuffs. She eats a couple of penis chocolates, concealing the pink-foil wrapper evidence in her purse instead of the trash can where Neeka might see it. She plays with a yellow feather boa for a while, and then tries on a pair of red, latex, knee-high boots that have been sitting on the shelf for months. The three-inch heels make her nearly six feet tall. She feels like the Amazon queen of the porn shop as she stomps around thinking how funny it would be (for a few reasons) if her parents walked in right then.

She had grown up with the sense that she was being conditioned for a climate-controlled life, expected to live contented in a storage box with an apron, a Book of Mormon, and a checkbox guide to salvation. First item on the list: don't climb out of the box. While trying to climb out of the box, she asked defiant questions that conflicted with all of the other check boxes. From recipes that called for cooking wine to what god to worship, she refused to believe their way was the only way. She was labeled a dissenter early, which angered and frightened her parents, threatened her religious peers, and challenged her elders. After years of emotional and physical abuse intended to subdue her, she finally shut them out—coming and going as she pleased, sometimes disappearing for days. Eventually, the standoff led to an epic standoff resulting in her being thrown out of her parents' home. But she'd left willingly. Three states away from where she spent the majority of her miserable childhood in Salt Lake City, Utah, she's been trying to create a life for herself near Seattle—close to an area where her family had lived briefly before moving back to Salt Lake City. Freed from the constraints of their religious ideals, Rachel has thrived. She had no trouble getting jobs, paying her own bills, and even less trouble forging her dad's signature, so she could take the GED to finish high school, and get better jobs. She didn't necessarily intend for her efforts to lead to a job that is so defiant of the narrow-minded ideals she was raised with, but it's definitely on her list of pros.

Realizing Neeka will be back any minute, she puts the shiny boots back on the shelf, and checks that nothing is out of place. When Neeka's car pulls into the parking lot, Rachel walks over to the DVDs and pulls a stack off the shelf, slides a bunch to the left, then puts *The Ten Cummandments* up front.

Neeka walks in looking refreshed. "Bummer, you beat me to it." She drops her coat and purse in the back room, then scans the store for another project.

"You were right, this shelf was a mess. It's taken me your whole break to reorganize it." Rachel puts the remaining DVDs back in a slightly different order, then walks behind the cash register.

Neeka hurriedly sorts the underwear bin, then leaves early

for a doctor appointment she apparently *forgot to mention.*

Foot traffic is slow in the entire shopping center for the rest of the afternoon, so Rachel just sits behind the front counter reading. Eventually, the bells on the door jingle, and she looks up in a daze, half expecting the downtrodden heroine in her book to be in need of sexy lingerie to seduce her sinewy gardener.

"Bad time?" Justin asks.

Rachel smiles. "Never."

He reaches into his brown corduroy jacket, pulls out a thick envelope of pictures, and lays it on the counter. Rachel flips through the stack, looking at each one intently. Squinting in disappointment at every shot, she hopes for something that will exonerate her for what, so far, appears to be a waste of a roll of film.

Justin waits impatiently. "Are you gonna leave me in suspense forever?"

Rachel gets excited by one of the photos, and quickly thumbs through the remaining few—all disappointing. She lays the good picture on the counter in front of Justin.

He squints, bending down for a closer look. "Just looks like a bunch of dots." He picks up the photo and carries it into brighter light. "Am I missing something?"

"They're orbs!" Rachel beams.

Justin looks confused.

"Balls of energy—like spirits caught on film."

He laughs.

"You don't believe in that stuff?"

"Spots are usually caused by the space between the lens and the built-in-flash decreasing the angle of light, causing

the light to reflect off of normally invisible particles. That—
or you had a spot on the lens."

"Then why aren't they in all my pictures?"

Justin shrugs.

Rachel snatches the photo out of his hand and walks back
behind the counter. "I've taken dozens of photos in this room
with different cameras, in different light, and I always get one
like this."

"Where is that?"

"My bedroom."

"Let me see it again." He holds out his hand.

She hesitates.

"Come on—I'll be nice, just let me see it."

"Do you even believe in ghosts?" she asks. Some of her
middle-dreams are so real she can't help but wonder. She
doesn't need him to buy an EMF reader or Ouija Board; she
just hopes he'll consider the possibility.

He thinks for a minute. "Sure, yeah—why not. I'd be more
shocked to find out they don't exist than that they do."

Rachel hands over the photograph.

"If this is your bedroom, and you think these are ghosts
or spirits or whatever, that's kinda creepy."

Rachel suddenly feels like she's divulging too much. She
doesn't want to seem crazy. "It's really not that big of a deal.
My friend, Sadie, and I go around to random places taking
photos like this for fun. It's just some kooky thing we do when
we're bored. You want to see her?" Rachel opens her wallet
and pulls out a folded photo of her and Sadie making goofy
faces.

"If I was a ghost, I would want to be in a photo with

two hot chicks like this lucky little orb." He reaches over the counter and picks up a red marker, drawing a heart around a small white spot in the bottom right corner of the photo, then hands it back to Rachel.

"This was also taken in my bedroom, by the way."

"I'm gonna have to see this mysterious bedroom of yours."

Rachel laughs to buffer the awkward silence.

"Are you working tomorrow?" Justin asks.

"Yep."

"Cool." The bells on the door jingle and he's gone.

Oh gawd, now he really thinks I'm a weirdy. She drives home in silence, ruminating over ways to counter his dust-on-the-lens theory.

Binding Spirits

Rachel opens her eyes. Moonlight penetrating cracks between the gauzy, floral-embroidered curtain panels isn't bright enough to illuminate her hazy purple bedroom. The haze indicates she's not completely awake yet, but she's still not able to cue herself to this fact while asleep—like the sleep disorder reference materials recommend.

She blinks, trying to improve her vision, but it doesn't help. A rush of panic comes with the realization that she can't move her arms. Her entire body is heavy, paralyzed. The growing pressure on her chest is suffocating. She gasps for air. Desperate to regain control, she tries to rock from side to side. No change. An obscure shadow bolts across the room. Fear forces her to react. Jolting forward, she awakes and reaches out. The purple haze is gone.

Heart pounding, preparing for the unknown, she pleads with an even greater unknown to keep her safe. She waits.

Nothing happens. Her heart slows, and the only sound comes from the metallic whirl of a fan blowing near the window. Removing one hand from beneath the blanket, she wipes small beads of sweat from her forehead. The outline of the dresser, shelves, and clothes strewn across the floor come slowly into focus. She glances at the clock—three more hours until her day begins.

Blue light emanates from the clock face on her bedside table. The polished surface of the white-gold cross she'd inherited from her grandmother a few years ago shimmers in the glow. The cross was left to Rachel's father, but after converting to Mormonism for her stepmother, all things Catholic were banned from their home, including Grandma. Rachel's stepmother sloughed the offensive piece of jewelry off on Rachel, but she's happy to have it. Instinctively, she reaches for it to chant one of the protection prayers her grandmother had taught her so many years ago, she can now barely remember. Though experience has taught her it's useless, she wishes she could go back to when she believed that was all she needed. Even after losing faith, its implied importance—depicted through shape alone, was more convincing hanging from her grandmother's neck. Dangling beneath a face creased with experience and wisdom it was impregnated with purpose. Now it just looks like a pile of beads and metal.

Pressing the lamp switch, the bulb sparks with life, makes a faint buzzing sound, blinks, then burns out. She struggles to untangle her legs from the warm blanket. Slowly navigating her way out of the bedroom, she wades through thick darkness to the other side of the living room. It takes longer than usual to locate the light switch, resulting in waves of panic. Finally, her fingers slide from the chalky surface of the wall to the smooth switch plate, and light overpowers dark, like a shield of armor.

Rachel stumbles to the couch. No television remote in sight, and she forgot to buy batteries—again, so there's no point in searching. She sits in silence, trying to focus on something positive. Just as she starts falling back to sleep, a rustling noise startles her. She looks down as Ewoka arches her back and rubs up against the front of the couch. Rachel leans down and scoops her up. Ewoka coos.

The alarm blares from the bedroom. She's queasy from lack of sleep. Digging her address book out of the nightstand drawer, she finds the number for her manager, groans a few times to make her voice sound scratchy, coughing for effect as her district manager—also half-asleep—picks up the phone. By the end of the conversation she sounds satisfactorily convinced that Rachel isn't well enough to work. Rachel opens the curtains to let in as much light as possible, and then climbs back into bed.

Anything Blue

The buzzing phone bouncing on the nightstand wakes Rachel. She barely misses catching it as it falls off and rolls under the bed. She finds the phone, along with a few lost hair ties, then bangs the back of her head on the windowsill. An aftershock shoots through her skull. She rubs the tender spot, hoping the blow won't leave a bump, looks at her call history, and wonders why Sadie had called five times. She checks voicemail—nothing—then calls her back.

"Oh my gawd! Where the hell have you been!?" Sadie screams into the phone.

Rachel holds the phone away from her ear. "I've been passed out all morning."

"I didn't hear from you last night, so I went by your *sex den* on my break this morning, and that annoying new girl said something about you being sick, then acted all suspicious when I looked shocked. I had to lie and say her shoes were fabulous just to negate suspicion, and then I had to sit through like a twenty-minute explanation of where she bought the stupid shoes, and by the time I left I had to go straight back to work. Anyway, I've been wondering what the hell is up. Seriously, Rach, if you're gonna call in sick you really need to text me or something."

"I figured you were busy with what's-his-name and hadn't noticed."

"Screw Todd! We broke up."

"And you didn't call me last night!?"

"It all went down crazy late, and then we got back together for like an hour. Until he pissed me off again and I threw him out. But he didn't leave until like three hours later. By then it was three-ish....So are you up for consoling your best friend tonight or not?"

"I suppose I could use a little memory loss. What's the plan?"

"It's a surprise. Be ready by seven. I'll pick you up."

Rachel checks for other missed calls or texts—nothing. Justin obviously doesn't miss her as much as Sadie misses her, and *why should he*. Rachel thinks about her sketchy history with guys, and how the two relationships she was the most invested in had both ended in disaster. But deep down, she feels like her growing friendship with Justin is different. He seems emotionally stronger than most of the guys she's known, but she doesn't have the strength to put him to the test—at least not this week, so she scraps the notion and prepares to get wasted.

Sadie arrives at almost eight—swearing she said seven-thirty. She smells like the perfume counter at a department store and looks ready to street-walk Broadway. Her box-bleach hair is straightened, and her gray eyes are masked in thick waves of silver-blue eyeshadow, matching the blue bra underneath her sheer white blouse. The tops of her black knee-high leather boots stop seven or eight inches below the hem of her black, pleated mini-skirt, and her bony knees are hidden beneath bright-white fishnet stockings.

"Like my necklace?" Sadie asks, fingering a shiny blue ball hanging from a black velvet ribbon. "I made it."

Rachel responds with exaggerated enthusiasm to avoid being asked repeatedly until Sadie feels she's elicited a worthy response. "I feel under-dressed. I wish you'd given me a heads up."

Sadie scans Rachel. "You always get numbers when you wear your faded jeans with the hole in the ass. Seriously, you look amazing. If I was into chicks I would take you right now."

Rachel hesitates to leave. "I don't know. Maybe I should change?"

Sadie leans forward, pulls down the front of Rachel's tight, green, low-cut top, exposing the black lace trim of her bra. Then she pushes her own breasts together, so her A-cups look closer to C's. "Now we're twins!"

Rachel laughs. "Where are we going?"

Sadie peels out of the parking lot in the two-year-old, black compact car her Dad had purchased as a college graduation present. It smells like cheeseburgers and cocoa-butter tanning lotion. Headlights reflect off the words

The Light in the Sound

SPEED HUMP on a yellow metal diamond. Sadie leans over the steering wheel, pointing up as they slowly roll over the *speed hump*. "One of these days I'm gonna steal that sign, so I can hang it in my room as a tribute to our fabulousness."

Rachel laughs.

"So after the breakup last night I woke up feeling very folk rock, but this outfit is all about fast riffs and angry drums— you agree?"

Rachel nods while staring into the vanity mirror. She feels plain, especially sitting next to the ice-blue princess. She thinks Cleopatra eyes look exotic with her dark hair and complexion, so she steadies her hand and brings her eyeliner out to a point with a slight upturn. Sitting back to assess her work, she just feels ridiculous.

Sadie reaches back to pull her iPod out of a large canvas bag on the backseat and travels into the middle lane. Another car swerves to avoid being sideswiped and honks.

"Holy shit! Just ask me—why don't you." Rachel pushes Sadie's arm out of the way.

Sadie sticks her tongue out and waves her middle finger at the driver of the honking car.

Rachel plugs the iPod into the stereo and selects an obscure Indie band she barely knows but Sadie loves. Music blares, and Sadie screams the lyrics to every song as Rachel tries to keep pace. One brief traffic jam, and nine songs later, Sadie turns down an alley, then pulls into the parking lot of a black brick building just south of downtown Seattle. Overhead, orange and yellow office lights polka-dot skyscrapers framed by the late evening twilight—a lavender and blue gradation that looks like a professional sketch on a child's Light-Up Drawing Pad. The energy of the city beckons. Rachel is disappointed as she scans the small dark building for a sign.

"This is supposed to be the best new club in town." Sadie gets out of the car and wiggles her skirt into place. "A guy at my work says his cousin comes here every Saturday."

Rachel is suspicious of the number of trucks parked in the poorly lit parking lot. "As long as it's not a sausage-fest."

"His cousin told him the ratio is great. And *supposedly* hot chicks don't have to pay a cover."

Rachel opens the door and steps into a puddle…"Shit!" She scowls at her mud-soaked boot.

Sadie laughs.

A cool, salty breeze from the nearby Sound blows empty cigarette packs and soggy taco stand wrappers around the parking lot. Rachel takes a deep breath and readjusts her studded belt. Sadie follows a group of people heading toward a side entrance. The group looks barely old enough to drive, or maybe that's just Rachel's perception because she feels too old for clubbing—but then she always had. Sneaking into places before she turned twenty-one, she'd rarely been carded, but never felt lucky to be there, just awkward, and would spend the night doing little more than what felt like playing the part her friends expected of her.

Rachel checks the car door locks and her cell for missed calls, then hustles to catch up with Sadie. A large guy with a crew-cut, who looks like he should be wearing fatigues and jogging in place while chanting a marching cadence, checks their IDs, stamps their hands, and lets them pass—no charge. He points to a room through an arched entrance at the end of a long green hallway.

Sadie asks, "Did you see if he charged anyone in front of us?"

"Yeah, he charged the girl with the purple Mohawk, and let the others in for free."

"Shut up! Really!?"

"Gawd no. Do you really think a club would be successful if they charged some girls in a group and not others? That would piss off so many people they'd have a charm-bracelet-army riot on their hands. They're obviously just letting all of the girls in for free."

Sadie looks less confident than she had five seconds earlier.

Rachel rolls her eyes.

Both girls stop below the arched entrance to a large dark room split into three sections: a bar, a dance floor, and an area with pool tables. Red, blue, and yellow spotlights zigzag on the dance floor where people gyrate in unison. The ratio of guys to girls is good, and there's a variety of people in all shapes and sizes. A little person—female—wearing black leather, assless chaps, and a checkered bustier, serves drinks to a group of young guys playing pool in the back. On the dance floor, a lanky guy with a mustache smiles at Rachel. She feels uncomfortably warm and follows a row of tables to the bar. Sadie is on her heels.

Rachel stares at the glow-in-the-dark stamp on the back of her hand: proof she's a member of the over-21 club. Smeared, fluorescent-yellow words read, "Drink Safely." She laughs. *What an oxymoron.* A ribbon of smoke wafts by her face, burning her eyes. The owner of the cigarette flicks ash on the floor, sticks the cigarette back in her mouth, picks up her drink and walks away. Rachel waves smoke away from her face and hopes the girl trips and chokes. Stepping up to the bar, "Give me something blue!" she yells over the music to a male bartender wearing a light-gray shirt that's two sizes too small and has a spray-tan stained collar. The shirt accentuates enough muscle that it wouldn't be worth scoffing at, had he not been trying so hard to show it off.

"Anything blue—no preference?" He flashes a wide row of bleached teeth at Rachel, breaks the horizon line, then fills a cup with ice, holding eye-contact for an uncomfortably long time.

She gets excited thinking he might like her, then remembers it's his *job* to like her. "Yeah, anything blue." She glances behind her, making sure Sadie hasn't wandered off.

He exchanges a bright-blue drink with a yellow umbrella for a ten-dollar bill, winking as he hands back her change. Rachel leaves two dollars on the bar, and steps aside for Sadie to order—careful not to make any unnecessary glances in his direction.

"Oooooh…I think he likes you," Sadie says.

"Doubtful." Rachel swallows a mouthful of the tangy concoction and tries to ignore the burn as it lights up her throat.

Sadie opens her mouth to respond. Instead, she screams, "Eric!" waving to a tall blonde who looks excited to see her.

Immediately, Rachel knows why they're here.

Sadie and Eric both blurt out some bullshit about being shocked to run into each other. A short, stocky guy with small, deep-set eyes stands behind Eric. He only acknowledges the group during a quick introduction. Rachel has already forgotten his name. She gulps down the remainder of her drink, and announces she's going back to the bar for another. Eric pauses from peering down the front of Sadie's blouse to suggest his friend go with her. Handing him a twenty-dollar bill, he asks him to bring back a couple of beers for him and Sadie as well.

Rachel signals Eric's crony, and heads back to the bar. She slows down to let her shadow catch up. "Sorry, what's your name again?"

"Dale."

She smiles and tries to make eye contact, which he avoids.

Instead, he stares at the sweaty beer bottle spinning in his palm. "Nice to meet you," he mutters.

She quickly sizes him up as not her type, which makes her more comfortable. "So be straight with me, Dale."

He looks nervous.

"They set this up, didn't they? They totally planned this shit. We're just here to make them look like they have friends, and to maybe even hook up with each other.

Dale laughs. He seems shocked by her candid assessment and relaxes a bit. "Pretty much."

"No worries. I have a boyfriend, so you're off the hook." Rachel lied about the boyfriend but felt justified as it being in Dale's best interest. She isn't the type to play a guy's ego for free beer, and this guy is too fragile to mess with. She wonders if there's a fun or intelligent guy hiding beneath the diffident exterior. Even so, physical attraction is too important. A long-term relationship can't be built on straight teeth alone, so she chalks him up as a new friend, at best.

Dale takes the blow-off well. Looking more relieved than

disappointed, he guzzles his beer.

"Give me something orange please," Rachel yells over the music to the bartender.

He smiles and shakes his head, fills a fresh glass with something peachy, and tops it off with a purple umbrella, pausing to draw a smiley face.

"You know any good drinking games?" Dale asks.

"Just drink every time Sadie says *shut-up* or *sparkle*."

He looks skeptical.

"Trust me; we'll be wasted in an hour."

"Shut up!" Sadie yells as they near the table.

Rachel raises her glass. "Hope you can hold your liquor." She takes a swig and gestures for Dale to drink up.

Two hours, four beers, one yellow drink, two red drinks, and a pile of umbrellas later, Rachel and Dale are wasted. Dale relaxes, and even does a silly dance. Inebriation fools her into thinking she might like him more than she'd initially thought, but then he says he doesn't like dogs, which is a deal breaker. Still, she's impressed by how he keeps his distance, and despite a few subtle advances, he never gets sloppy or aggressive. Sadie and Eric, on the other hand, remain sober while talking, and occasionally slow dance with their faces smashed together so tight Rachel thinks Eric may swallow Sadie. Finally, Dale complains about needing to get up early for work. Eric reluctantly agrees to leave, but only if Sadie will go out with him again—alone next time.

"Yes, please, alone," Rachel thinks, drunkenly aloud.

Sadie scowls.

Rachel and Dale stand in the parking lot awkwardly waiting for Eric and Sadie to finish their goodbye face suck.

Dale stares at the ground and fidgets with his jacket. Rachel leans in to give him a hug and runs into his face. He quickly reciprocates, and before she can retract, her mouth is filled with his beer and onion breath. His tongue is thick and doesn't fit in her mouth. Rachel feels like she's suffocating and has to back up for air. It's a welcome release from the pity gesture she's already regretting. She slurs something about not feeling well, then rushes over to Sadie's car to wait alone while the last red drink still has so much influence over her.

"Isn't Eric fabulous!" Sadie yells as she jumps into the car. "A real dreamboat."

"What's your damage?" Sadie swerves to avoid a pothole in the road.

Rachel's shoulder slams into the car door. "Watch it!" She braces herself on the "oh-shit" bar. "You better slow-the-hell-down if you don't want puke in your car."

"Well?"

"What do you *think* is wrong?!" Rachel scowls. "You blindsided me with Romeo and his beady-eyed sidekick. I thought we were having a girls-night-out to mourn the loss of what's-his-name."

"Todd!"

"Whatever! Remembering his name is obviously not worth my energy."

"I should have told you about Eric, but I was afraid you wouldn't come, and I really needed you here! Anyway, it doesn't look like the night was a total loss." Sadie points to a small umbrella with a scribbled phone number that Rachel has been twirling since leaving the bar. "Looks like you and

Dale hit it off pretty well." She giggles.

"That's the bartender's number."

"Holy shit—score!"

"Yeah, yeah—he was flirting with a bunch of other girls, too. Sorry, pretty-boy isn't my type."

"You need to lighten up." Sadie rolls down her window and hangs her head out. "Sooo, what did you think of Eric?"

"I think he's crazy hot and perfect for you. I think you should marry him, live happily ever after, and pop out a bunch of Hitler's poster children."

"If you weren't drunk I'd be pissed."

"No, really. I think he's great. I hope it works out swimmingly." Rachel makes swimming motions in the air.

Sadie groans. "Can I crash at your place tonight? My mom is being a beast, and I don't want her to know I was out so late, and drinking."

Rachel sighs and lies her head back, pretending to be asleep for the rest of the ride home.

Jesus Not Penus!

"Jesus Not Penus! Jesus Not Penus! Jesus Not Penus!" Three picketers, holding what Rachel hopes are purposely misspelled signs, march back and forth on the sidewalk chanting as she unlocks the door to the porn shop.

"Jesus had a penis—you're an idiot if you think he never used it!" Rachel yells back.

The homely girl in the middle gasps. "I will pray for you!" She waives her sign erratically, either on the verge of a seizure or trying to cleanse the air.

Rachel points, "You have to pray over there because the parking lot is private property. If you don't move out to the city-owned grass I'm gonna call the cops."

A tall, skinny kid with bright-red hair steps forward. "Sinner!"

"Thirty seconds!" Rachel flips him off and walks inside.

She turns on the lights, and preps to start the day, pausing only once to make sure they moved out of the parking lot. It's been months since she's seen any protestors, but they usually show up close to Easter, so she isn't shocked. Each time it's a new group of wide-eyed kids, eager to impress their pastor and Bible-thumping friends.

The bells on the door jingle, and Justin walks in grinning. "Looks like you have some fans today."

"We met."

"You want me to get rid of them?"

"It's cool. Around lunch they're gonna get nailed with trash and ketchup packets by people driving by."

"Oh gawd, why do they do it?"

"Picket or throw ketchup?"

"Picket. I *get* the ketchup."

"Didn't you get the memo? Salvation costs a happy-meal's worth of trash to the side of the head these days."

"Maybe I should warn them."

"Nah, they'll be so excited to wear their ketchup-stained shirts to youth group tomorrow they'll barely sleep tonight."

"Sounds like you've had experience."

"I was raised oober religious. We used to accost the so-called sinners going to R-rated movies. I've had my share of condiment-stained clothing."

"If they could see you now."

Rachel curtsies next to a wall of fetish wear.

"Screw porn. I always wonder about profanity cuz it's different in every country. Take England for example—there, bitchin' isn't profane, but here it is. And the word crap isn't profane here, but there it is. Does that mean I can spend my whole life swearing and not go to hell if I die in England?"

"As long as you switch your citizenship—I'm guessing it's all about the paperwork."

Justin laughs. "So where were you Saturday? I thought you were working."

"Out with friends."

"Oh sure, go do something fun and don't invite me. That's cool. I see how it is." He attempts to pout, but just looks gay.

"Weren't you busy with your bro's doing something frat-party-ish anyway?"

"Hardly, I spent the weekend doing homework."

"Sorry."

"I'm so close to graduating, it's not so bad anymore."

Rachel has no idea what it would be like to complete any major life accomplishment. Screw college, she'd missed the opportunity to be a kid and even graduate high school because she was so preoccupied escaping her parents' abuse and instability. Afterward, survival became top priority. She'd never really considered going back to school. Time constraints—and lack of money—prevented college from ever being a viable option.

"You should try to get some government grants. It's a sure thing if you're married and broke, but I don't have enough money to take you to Vegas this weekend, so you're on your own."

"No worries, I don't say *I do* on the first date."

"Speaking of which, it probably would have seemed more *cool* if I'd waited until like Thursday or something, but I hate all the dating game shit, so you wanna do something this weekend?" The color rushes out of Justin's face. Even if

Rachel had a million things planned that weekend she would have canceled it all.

"I should probably *play it cool* and say I need to check my schedule then call you later, but I'm not good at games either, so we should definitely do something."

"I don't have much money, but my friend's band is doing a show on Saturday night, and he said he can get us into the place for free. Then we could drive around town and look for people to throw ketchup packets at."

Rachel laughs. "Sounds fun."

The bells on the door jingle, and a tall, slim police officer walks in. The small black plastic square attached to his shoulder beeps then hisses.

"Can I help you?" Rachel asks. She'd seen a few customers pull into the parking lot driving police cruisers, though they never came in uniform. They were always plain-clothed and usually looking for penis pumps. Given the uniform, she expects him to be looking for a last-minute gift—probably lingerie—for a girlfriend or wife, so she points toward a sale rack.

"I need to speak with the person in charge."

"Is there a problem?"

Putting his hand on his belt, his left thumb caresses the gun holster. The extra padding of bulletproof vest prevents his arms from hanging freely at his sides, creating a conveniently intimidating stance. Rachel pictures the geeky hall-monitor she'd punched in the stomach in third grade for not letting her go to the bathroom without a pass. The officer's young, insecure face has *test me* written all over it. And even though she's not intent on punching him in the stomach, she wishes she could flick him on the nose and tell him to be nice.

"We've had some complaints from other shop owners in the complex regarding a group of people walking around the parking lot with signs that say *penis*. Are they advertising for this shop?"

"Did you bother to read their signs? They're protesting."

"Have you asked them to leave?"

"Yes."

"Are you aware that displaying a sign that says *penis* is a public disturbance?"

"Shouldn't you be telling *them* that?"

"I have every intention of talking to them, but it's *your* responsibility to oversee all things pertaining to this shop."

"Are you trying to blame me for a bunch of bored kids—I've never met in my life—deciding to picket the shop?"

"You should have called it in."

"I'll remember that next time. In the meantime, I'll put up a sign that says *no penis signs allowed.*"

Justin laughs.

"Do you think this is a joke, Miss?" the officer asks.

"I just think you're talking to the wrong person."

"I'll talk to them, but if you have any more problems I expect you to call it in."

"Sure," she says, holding up the basket on the counter, "Complimentary penis-chocolate, officer?"

He pauses, looks around the shop, sizes Justin up, shakes his head, then turns to leave.

Justin gives the middle finger to his back. "I guess I better get back to work. Unfortunately, it's gonna be a long day because I think it already peaked."

"What time Saturday?"

He smiles. "I'll call you."

"Oh sure, *now* you play it cool."

 Throwing Ketchup

$\mathcal{R}$achel expects Justin to arrive any minute. She checks to make sure nothing is stuck between her teeth or sticking out of her nose. Headlights fill the front window. She races through the bedroom and bathroom one last time to ensure no worn underwear or bras are embarrassingly visible. Justin knocks. Ewoka jumps off the couch and runs out of the living room. Part of Rachel wishes she could follow.

"Right on time!" She smiles and motions him in.

Justin smells delicious, like cinnamon and apple pie. He takes the liberty of giving himself a tour of her apartment. He seems anxious to learn as much about her as possible. She's relieved he didn't linger in the living room, making awkward small talk. He pauses to examine the black and white photographs of city bridges in the hallway, hanging on the one wall in the apartment she had painted black to contrast with the photos.

"Did you take these?"

"Yeah."

"They're really good!"

"Painting is really my thing."

"Do you have anything I can see?"

She leads him into her bedroom and picks up a couple of canvases—unfinished paintings of dead trees and winged women.

He laughs, pointing at a caricature Rachel had drawn of Sadie that's propped in the corner.

Rachel frowns.

"Oh—sorry—no—those are really great."

She is unimpressed with the penitent compliment and wishes she'd never shown him anything.

"So, this is the infamous haunted bedroom?" He stares up at the ceiling, as if expecting Slimer from *Ghostbusters* to appear any moment. "Take any new spooky pictures lately?"

"Spirit photography dates back like 140 years, you know. I'm really not that weird. Sure, there are some whopping hoaxes out there, but it's considered to be one of the few, if not only, scientifically credible ways to prove the existence of an afterlife."

"Have you ever caught a recognizable ghost in a photograph—something other than just a ball of light—or what did you call it...an orb?"

Rachel opens the bottom drawer of her dresser, pulling out a stack of her best ghost photo-bombs, thumbs through the group, and hands three to Justin. The first is a photo of her sitting on the kitchen counter at a friend's house. A large, orange and yellow mass of spider-webbed light hovers next to her.

Justin examines the picture, then goes to the next photo of a scowling, middle-aged woman in a long, floral dress holding a Bible. "Who's this evil bitch?"

Rachel laughs. "My stepmother."

"No offense."

"It's cool, none taken—pretty astute actually. She was pissed at me that day because you're not supposed to take pictures inside the church." Rachel points to the blurry image of what almost appears to be a person standing behind her stepmother. "I'm guessing that's why you're not allowed to take photos."

"Yeah, they don't want you stealing their souls." Justin laughs.

The most convincing photo is of what seems to be a diaphanous man leaning over Rachel while she's sleeping.

"My ex-boyfriend took that picture. He might have photo-shopped it to fuck with me—he was a dick like that. But if it's legit, it's a good one."

Justin looks disturbed.

"You can run away screaming now if you want—I'll totally understand."

"Nah, just remind me to bring my Proton-pack if I ever spend the night."

"Oh, you think you have a chance of getting that far?" Rachel pokes him in the side.

"Well, I'm not running away screaming. That has to give me an edge over at least a couple of guys."

She laughs, but it's frustratingly true.

Justin unlocks the passenger door of his truck and offers her a hand as she leaps up onto the seat. She leans over and unlocks his door. He nods in appreciation, and she knows she scored points. The sun has just set, and the Prussian-blue sky is obstructed by only a few wisps of charcoal-gray cloud. The cool night air rustles tree limbs. A few leaves fall, and she resists the impulse to get out and twirl in the parking lot. Instead, she hangs her arm out the window and lets the wind roll through her fingers.

He takes the long way through winding back roads lined with moonlit conifers rising from the forest floor blanketed with ferns. Pulling into the parking lot of a log-cabin style building covered in neon beer lights, he parks near the front entrance. A young couple runs up to the truck, then two more people rush out of the building. Justin introduces his friends as Kaleb, Abbie, Ian, and Cerise. Rachel feels all eight eyes scrutinizing her. Ian has dark brown hair, and a distinct scar above his left eye. It's so pronounced that on most guys, it would be off-putting, but with his muscular physique and tendency to fidget, she assumes it happened during a daredevil stunt that makes a great party anecdote. Kaleb is a baby-faced, sandy-blond with shaggy hair, and seems laid back. He looks like he should be riding a surfboard not standing in a gravel parking lot surrounded in pine trees. Either way, the short, curly-haired girl with small, perky, braless breasts hanging on his arm makes sense.

Cerise is in her own universe. Rachel can't help noticing how distracted she seems while Justin does introductions. Her eyes dart, then fixate on something until she rules out a reason to pounce, like an owl on a branch hunting at dusk. She doesn't seem to be with Ian, and other than being stunning, Rachel can't figure out where Cerise belongs in the group. It's fifty-degrees, yet she's standing outside in nothing but a tight black tank top and doesn't seem cold. In fact, her creamy cocoa skin is radiating heat. Her thick, sandy-brown hair has blonde highlights, and is ironed straight. Her flawless complexion requires minimal makeup, and shimmering white eyeliner makes her pale-green eyes sparkle. Her porn-star curves and plump, pink-glossed lips have *fuck-me* written all over them. Rachel can't compete with this girl. She's nervous and coughs.

"You okay?" Justin puts his hand on her shoulder.

"My throat's dry."

"She needs a beer! C'mon we've got a pitcher." Cerise waves her arms toward the building, and seems buzzed, if not already drunk.

"Cerise—that's a cool name," Rachel says.

Cerise slams down a shot, then shoves a lime in her mouth. "Thanks," she mumbles through green rind. She sucks the lime out and puckers her lips. "It's a shade of pink. My parents were crazy hippies. Mom is an astrologer, my Dad is an artist, and I'm a masseuse. What about you and yours?"

"My dad's a dick, my stepmother's vying to become Jesus' whore, and I work in a porn shop."

Cerise has a boisterous, guttural laugh, and pounds her fist on the table. "Holy shit—I like you. I like her," she repeats to Justin.

"How many has she had?" Justin asks.

"Like five shots and one beer." Kaleb glances toward Rachel and makes a goofy face while pointing at Cerise.

"Blah, blah, blah—I'm fine." Cerise waves her hand in the air and orders another shot. "Come on, girly—you need to catch up." She hands Rachel a beer, prompting her to drink.

Rachel chugs, and everyone looks impressed.

"Don't listen to these alchie's," Justin says. "They'll knock ya on your ass."

"I can hold my own." Rachel winks.

Cerise grabs Rachel's hand. "It's time for palm readings!" she announces loud enough for the whole bar to hear.

Abbie seems annoyed by Cerise hoarding everyone's attention; she grabs Kaleb's hand and drags him to the jukebox.

Cerise rolls her eyes and grips Rachel's hand tighter. Attempting an Italian-gypsy accent, she says, "Now you just sit back and let Madame Cerise predict your future." She rolls Rachel's hand palm up, and traces lines with her finger for so long Rachel finishes half a beer. Cerise lets out a long sigh. "You see…you seeeeeeeeee—"

Rachel thinks Cerise might actually be sensing something about her. "I see?"

"You seeeeee…what I'm saying!" Cerise throws Rachel's hand down and cackles, then picks up her beer and watches Rachel intently through squinted eyes while gulping.

Cerise can't sit still during the show, and dances with nearly everyone, never taking her eyes off Justin & Rachel for longer than a moment. Rachel finds her childlike, erratic energy magnetic, and senses it's more than just being drunk. Cerise is passionate and comfortable in her own skin—traits Rachel admires.

The drums are an ideal outlet for Ian's jittery energy.

The Light in the Sound

Midway through the show, one of his sticks breaks and a jagged shard nails him in the forehead, causing a thin stream of blood to run down his nose—likely the origin of his eyebrow scar. Rachel leaves to find the restroom, and Cerise follows. She squeezes into the same stall as Rachel and props herself in the corner, trying not to fall over. Rachel feels uncomfortable peeing with an audience.

"You know I was really scared to meet you. Justin keeps raaaaving to everyone about how cool you are, and I just couldn't bear you not liking me."

"Well, I think you're fabulous."

"Really!" Cerise says, stumbling forward.

Rachel jumps off the toilet to catch her, and Cerise crumples into Rachel's arms. She smells like hops and strawberry lip-gloss. Their noses rub, and she kisses Rachel's cheek. "I think I love you."

Rachel laughs and props Cerise on her shoulder, so she can reach down to button her own pants.

"You're my new best friend. Will you marry me?" she says, slurring something else about also loving licorice.

Rachel helps her out of the bathroom, then tells Justin that Cerise is done for the night.

Cerise gives everyone hugs as they leave, except for one stranger who she throws a ketchup bottle at for not dancing with her.

He's slumped over drunk in the corner, and barely notices as the plastic bottle bounces off his shoulder.

Ian shakes his head.

Justin and Kaleb help Cerise into the back of Abbie's white Volkswagen rabbit.

Cerise collapses on a pile of clothes into instant slumber, as if drowning in the intensity of her own emotions.

"So, what's Cerise's story?" Rachel asks as Justin pulls out of the parking lot.

"Shit—you got all night?" Justin laughs. "She used to be with Ian, but she cheated on him and they broke up. She threatened to kill herself and they got back together, but then he cheated on her. She slashed the girl's tires, and smashed Ian's windshield with a bat, but they worked it out and ended up friends with benefits—know what I mean?"

"Ah."

"She's pretty messed up."

"I like her. She's spontaneous and unfiltered. Not guarded and reserved like most people."

"Or crazy—but your positive spin is refreshing." Justin smiles and pulls off onto a dirt road.

"She's *your* friend."

"I didn't know she was gonna be there tonight. Ian must have wanted a quicky before the show."

Rachel stares out over the cliff Justin parked dangerously close to and admires the view. The moon is full and illuminates the scene with striking clarity. Rows of silhouette pine trees framed by a black-onyx backcloth fill the horizon. An ethereal mist blankets the shortest treetops, crowning the rolling hillside stretching into an evergreen abyss.

Justin jumps out of the truck and stares into the blackness below. "I wonder how deep it is?"

Rachel shivers and folds her arms. She can smell a campfire in the distance and wishes she was near it.

He moves closer and pulls her inside his wool-lined,

corduroy jacket. Her stomach tightens. She wraps her arms around his waist. She knows she shouldn't let the alcohol influence her, but she needs him to want her, and she wants him to know how much she needs him. He leans down to kiss her; his lips brush hers, and she loses her balance, falling into him. She'd blame the alcohol, but a rock had come loose under her boot. She laughs, and Justin asks if she's okay. She nods and kisses *him* this time. Hard. They barely separate as they slowly make their way back into his truck. Once safely inside, kissing becomes petting and their hands occasionally collide in fevered exploration. She fears the emotional backlash of drunken sex. But it's been months since she's been touched below the waist by anything other than cold, Chinese silicone. She practically tears the button off Justin's jeans as she pulls off his pants and climbs on top of him. If anyone will be held accountable for subsequent guilt it will be her, she'll make sure of it.

Justin pauses. "This is going pretty fast. I'm cool if you wanna wait."

He sounds and looks so sincere it only makes her want him more. She knows better. Yet she hopes life is presenting her an opportunity for emotional ablution. Being in his arms is like going back to a place when unknowing was still a part of her identity. She feels protected from the past by the embrace of the boy she had a crush on in junior high, before relationships were hindered by fear and adult expectation for commitment and resolution. He reminds her of a time before her family cast her out for developing an awareness that insisted she turn her back on their antiquated God. He takes her back to before she forgot what it felt like to hope for the kind of emotion that transcends expectation that just *is* for the sake of *being*, without question. Most importantly, he takes her to a time before Derek. She prays that if anyone can free her from that emotional demon it will be Justin. Even if she never sees him again, she has to have him now. It's all or nothing. He pulls her closer and thrusts himself deep inside her. She gasps. Her body is flush with warmth and beads of sweat begin to soak through her shirt. She pulls off her top, burying his face between her breasts. Digging her nails into the back of his neck, she throws her head back and cries out, "Yes," during climax. Just before he comes, he wraps his arms around her and moans, "You feel amazing." But then it's over.

Justin looks adorable with flushed cheeks and sex hair, but they're both awkwardly silent for most of the ride home. As the mile markers whiz by, memories she's been suppressing for nine years surface. Like foam collecting on a pond during a heavy storm, no matter how hard she scrapes, it just keeps getting thicker. Justin squeezes her hand and smiles. He pulls into the parking lot of her apartment complex, gives her a kiss goodbye, promises to call the next day, then waits to see that she gets inside safely. She lets out a sigh of relief as he leaves. But as his distracting embrace drives further away, she wishes he would turn around and come back. Her apartment is dark and lonely. Drowning in memories, she fears she made a horrible mistake. Waves of nausea, coupled with severe agitation, make her want to slam her head through the wall. Instead, she gulps down four Aspirin then goes to bed.

Walk into My Parlour

Rachel avoids staring at the inside of the toilet. No matter how often she scrubs it, the white porcelain she puts her bare ass on to defecate should never be this close to her face. The sight of it increases her stomach convulsions. Drunk sex with Justin was the first time in years she had let her guard down while inebriated, and it was wonderful in the moment but is about to result in the same outcome as before. Even though alcohol makes her feel normal, and sex makes her feel wanted, the combination is too painful a reminder. Nine years have passed, but the memories of Derek and rape are still vivid, and difficult to replace with calming thoughts. The most painful memories are of having no one to turn to, and humiliation for trusting him. She couldn't forgive herself for letting her guard down and losing control over her own body. She was only fifteen, but she'd already had sex.

Moving every six months made her the new girl at school more often than she could count without a pen and paper. She was tired of being a social leper. No matter how many ways she reinvented herself, nothing increased her social currency like being sexually active. But where, when, and with whom, had been her choice, until Derek.

Before obscuring the truth beneath suppression and denial, Rachel's parents had put most of the blame on *her* for hanging out with the *wrong* crowd, and the rest of the blame on the color of Derek's skin. But Rachel could care less if he was blue and from another planet. White, black, red or yellow—ignorant, insecure, power-hungry men of any race will debase, humiliate, and subjugate women. His social-status also played into it. He was tall, muscular, and popular. He was on the football team, and he was surrounded by cheerleaders. Rachel felt so lucky to be the recipient of his attention she failed to be alarmed by how aggressive it was. He got angry when she wasn't home to take his calls. He liked to push her around, wrestle her to the ground, and laugh at her feeble attempts to defend herself. Finally, one Friday night, he took her to a party and got her wasted.

She was too drunk to go home, so he convinced her to spend the night with him and some other people at a friend's house, whose parents were out of town. She was wary but didn't dare face her parents while intoxicated. The other couple disappeared into an upstairs bedroom. Derek took Rachel downstairs to a small room with a concrete floor and little more than a bed. She could barely walk without falling and thanked him for the help. She slumped down on the bed and told him she felt like puking. He pointed to the bathroom.

The Light in the Sound

He was quieter than usual, fatherly as he helped take off her shoes. She fell sideways on the bed, trying to suppress waves of nausea. He walked around to the other side of the bed, gripped her shoulder, rolling her toward him, like a spider wrapping its prey in silk bands. She thanked him for finding her a place to crash. He kissed her. She reciprocated, but it didn't last. She stumbled to the bathroom, barely reached the toilet in time, vomiting what felt like every ounce of liquid in her stomach.

She hoped he would be asleep when she returned and hadn't heard her puking, but he was awake and looked agitated. His shirt was off, and he propped himself up on one arm. She climbed back into bed and told him she was sorry she didn't feel well and just needed sleep. He kissed her forcefully. His chest muscles flexed under her palms as she resisted. He scowled. She insisted she was too sick for anything to happen. Reenacting one of their play-fight wrestling matches, he swung his leg over her waist, hoisted his body on top of her, and pinned her arms. She promised if he waited that their first time would be soon, but his mind was made-up. She pleaded with him to stop. He unbuttoned and removed her pants with one hand—the other pinning both of hers. Reaching over the side of the bed toward a longneck can for a swig of the beer he'd been nursing the whole way home, she got enough room to lift her leg and center her foot on his chest. A surge of adrenalin coursing through one of the largest muscles in her body threw him to the floor. The bed slid backward. Metal wheels screeched on cold concrete. The mattress bulged like a windblown web. He stood up without pause, jumped on top of her, and punched her in the face. A slow pain coursed through her skull. The marshmallow skin surrounding her eye split open. Blood amalgamated tears; muddying, what Derek's defense attorney later referred to as, "Intimate details necessary to corroborate a credible story." Rachel leaned over the side of the bed and violently expelled the remainder of the alcohol and trust-in-men that she had left, while Derek expelled the fragmented remainder of his soul. Moments later, less time than it took to overpower her, it was over. A molt of the Derek, Rachel thought she knew— if he ever really existed—scurried away in search of more beer. She crawled into the bathroom, locking the door behind her.

Years later, the awareness of her own fragility still makes her sicker than alcohol ever does. She vowed never to put herself in a position where that could happen again. Even though Justin had already begun earning her trust, the pressure she feels between her legs, coupled with the taste and scent of alcohol on her breath, brings it all flooding back. She cries and vomits until dry-heaves cripple her abdomen.

The Spider and the Fly
Mary Howitt (1799-1888)

"Will you walk into my parlour?" said the Spider to the Fly,
  "Tis the prettiest little parlour that ever you did spy;
    The way into my parlour is up a winding stair,
      And I've a many curious things to shew when you are there."

"Oh no, no," said the little Fly, "to ask me is in vain,
For who goes up your winding stair
    -can ne'er come down again."

"I'm sure you must be weary, dear, with soaring up so high;
Will you rest upon my little bed?" said the Spider to the Fly.
"There are pretty curtains drawn around; the sheets are fine and thin,
And if you like to rest awhile, I'll snugly tuck you in!"

"Oh no, no," said the little Fly, "for I've often heard it said,
They never, never wake again, who sleep upon your bed!"

Said the cunning Spider to the Fly, "Dear friend what can I do,
  To prove the warm affection I've always felt for you?
    I have within my pantry good store of all that's nice;
      I'm sure you're very welcome — will you please to take a slice?"

"Oh no, no," said the little Fly, "kind Sir, that cannot be,
I've heard what's in your pantry, and I do not wish to see!"

"Sweet creature!" said the Spider, "you're witty and you're wise!
How handsome are your gauzy wings, how brilliant are your eyes!

I've a little looking-glass upon my parlour shelf,
  If you'll step in one moment, dear, you shall behold yourself."

"I thank you, gentle sir," she said, "for what you're pleased to say,
And bidding you good-morning now, I'll call another day."

The Spider turned him round about, and went into his den,
For well he knew the silly Fly would soon come back again:
So he wove a subtle web, in a little corner sly,
And set his table ready to dine upon the Fly.

Then he came out to his door again, and merrily did sing
  "Come hither, hither, pretty Fly, with the pearl and silver wing;
    Your robes are green and purple — there's a crest upon your head;
      Your eyes are like the diamond bright, but mine are dull as lead!"

Alas, alas! how very soon this silly little Fly,
Hearing his wily, flattering words, came slowly flitting by;
With buzzing wings she hung aloft, then near and nearer drew,
Thinking only of her brilliant eyes, and green and purple hue —
Thinking only of her crested head — poor foolish thing!

At last,
Up jumped the cunning Spider, and fiercely held her fast.
He dragged her up his winding stair, into his dismal den,
Within his little parlour — but she ne'er came out again!

And now dear little children, who may this story read,
To idle, silly flattering words, I pray you ne'er give heed:
Unto an evil counsellor, close heart and ear and eye,
And take a lesson from this tale, of the Spider and the Fly.

Social Currency

Rachel's cell phone chime rescues her from restless sleep. She peels her face from the warm, drool-soaked pillow. Harsh, midday sun prevents her from fully opening her eyes. "Hello?" she whispers to prevent the throbbing behind her corneas from traveling to the back of her skull.

An unfamiliar female voice replies, "Hello—who's this?"

"You called me."

She giggles. "This is Cerise. I'm trying to find Rachel.

"It's me."

"You sound like shit. I hope you don't look like shit."

"Why? Am I on a hidden camera show?"

"Yeah, don't look in your closet because a guy with balloons and a camcorder is about to jump out and yell surprise."

Rachel laughs. Her aching ribs resist.

"I got your number from Justin this morning. He said you

two were out late and made me promise I wouldn't call until I gave you enough time to sleep. How'd I do?"

The clock face is obstructed by blanket, but she can see the first number is a two. "Good. I should have been up hours ago." Rachel wonders if Justin told Cerise they had sex, but hopes he isn't the type of guy to fuck and vaunt, and she doesn't want to say anything that will result in finding out otherwise.

"Hangover?"

Rachel groans.

"Probably my fault—I don't remember much, which is part of why I'm calling. I always end up doing something when I'm drunk that I have to apologize for, so I just assume it's a given."

"No apology necessary."

"I don't believe you, but thanks." Cerise laughs—deep and breathy—filling the silence.

Rachel thinks Cerise may be trying to apologize for the bathroom thing, but she doesn't want to give her the opportunity. Rachel's had her own share of embarrassing drunk moments, and it's exciting to think Cerise might like her as more than just a friend. At the very least, it's a hell of a compliment. Rachel never gave much thought to being with a girl, other than fantasies. She'd always been drawn to guys, but the realization that she could get a girl as attractive as Cerise feels pretty good. It's like winning something expensive she never knew she wanted in a contest she never entered. Had it not happened, she never would have known what she was missing, but if Cerise reneges now it will be an upsetting loss.

55

"My Dad has an art show at a gallery downtown tonight. And last night—somewhere between my eighth shot and dancing with the pirate—I remember you saying you paint, and I thought you might want to come?"

"I don't think I'd be very good company right now."

"Oh, come on! You know you don't want to spend all night hanging out with the voyeur in the closet."

The conceivable truth in the connotation makes Rachel uneasy.

"Plus, if you don't come I'm gonna have to call pirate-guy, and you wouldn't wish that on me—would you?"

"I guess if it will save you from Blackbeard."

Cerise squeals. "Awesome! It will be superfun—I promise." Cerise hangs up before Rachel can change her mind.

She fears meeting Cerise's family. She dreads first impressions because parents never like her. She decides to lie about working in a porn shop, but remembers she already told Cerise the truth, so the best plan is to avoid that question altogether. Rachel has three missed calls, one from Justin, two from Sadie. She hears Justin's voicemail, and returns his call, leaving a message with a promise to call back after she gets home from the art show with Cerise.

Rachel counts the remaining sticks of gum in her purse, speed-blinks through three drops of Visine in each eye, and then enters the brightly-lit gallery. Rows of paintings fill whitewashed brick walls. Champagne glasses clink, and a waiter with stuffed mushrooms unknowingly grazes Rachel's left breast with the tray. She brushes away the sensation and two pieces of lint. Suddenly, the clothes that felt fabulous at home seem all wrong. If she were more like Sadie, she'd have half her wardrobe in the trunk, accessible at a moment's notice. Pushing her skirt down as low as possible and cuffing the sleeves of her black blouse will have to do.

Rachel waves to Cerise who races across the gallery, welcoming her with a hug. "You look fabulous!" Cerise reaches for the large chunk of green malachite in Rachel's necklace and gushes.

"So do you!" It's intended to be polite, but Rachel really means it. Equilibrium does wonders for Cerise. She also hadn't straightened her hair this time, and the large, naturally springy curls accentuate her bouncy demeanor. She had drunk twice as much alcohol as Rachel the night before yet shows no signs of hangover. Rachel hopes she put enough concealer over the puffy-pink bags under her own eyes and keeps smiling to avoid looking droopy.

"C'mon—I want you to meet my family!" Cerise squeezes Rachel's hand, pulling her toward the rear of the gallery. Unfamiliar faces zoom by. Rachel hopes to catch a glimpse of Cerise's parents before they size her up, but a round woman with frizzy, gray hair jumps in front of Cerise and demands a hug. Cerise reciprocates with locked elbows and a strained smile.

The woman points at her pasty-white knee covered in a purple vine of varicose veins. "I've known her since she was this tall," she says.

Cerise smiles and ushers the woman to the wine table where she hands Rachel a glass, then resumes course.

"Who was that?"

Cerise shrugs. "She comes to all of my dad's art shows. But if you have a conversation with her for more than a few minutes she starts calling you *Georgette* and plays an imaginary piano."

Rachel glances back at the strange woman who is now twirling in the corner, turning back around just in time to avoid running into Cerise's mother. An earthy woman with long, thick, auburn hair, and a ring on each finger, cups both of her hands over Rachel's hand. She leans forward. Three of her necklaces jingle like a wind chime. She speaks softly. "It's so lovely to meet you, Rachel. Cerise has been telling us all about what a wonderful time you both had at Ian's show last night."

"I should kick Justin for not introducing us sooner," Rachel says.

"Heaven's no, you've known each other for centuries," Cerise's mom says with a wink.

Rachel hopes she'll elaborate, but instead introduces Cerise's siblings. One arm around Cerise's younger sister, and the other around her older brother, she looks like a mother hen with outstretched wings. She forms a circle with her children, allowing Rachel to fill the gap. Cerise's dad, Ryley, edges in. Rachel thinks it's unusual that Cerise introduces him by name, but assumes it has something to do with the professional setting. He has pale gray eyes, and the striped transitions of his silver and brown hair speckled with gold reminds Rachel of hawk feathers.

"Thanks so much for inviting me," Rachel says.

"Cerise tells us you're an artist," he says.

Rachel is surprised. She's never been referred to as an artist before, and she'd never identified herself as one. Artist was something she didn't have to hide from or be ashamed of, but it also felt like a stretch. Rachel's few paintings and sketchpad propped against her dresser, pales in comparison to a gallery full of work representing years of dedication and experience. As much as she can sense about other people, she senses very little about herself, and fears that striving for something so spectacular will just end in disappointment. "I take photos, sketch, and paint sometimes, but it's nothing to brag about."

"We all have to start somewhere." He smiles, puts his hand on Rachel's shoulder and squeezes, then excuses himself to mingle with his guests.

Cerise's family members all seem like genuinely confident, self-aware people who don't just wait for their turn to speak; they listen intently and respond thoughtfully. They're the type of people who invigorate and inspire, rather than drain everyone's energy with complaints, demands, and judgments. By now, Rachel's family would have come up with multiple ways to snub Cerise. They would have made a crass joke at the expense of Rachel's character, and by the end of the night would have found a private moment to tell Cerise that she should stay away from Rachel altogether.

Rachel feels like crying until she glances up and notices the life-sized nude painting of Cerise's mom. She can't attest to the accuracy of the Florida-shaped birthmark on her inner thigh, but the auburn hair, deep-set round eyes, and Greek nose are very telling. Cerise's cheeks flush, and she ushers Rachel away from the painting. Rachel pictures Cerise as a child, embarrassed to bring friends' home because of her naked mother framed above the fireplace. For the first time that night, Rachel is glad she came.

Cerise makes the rounds, introducing Rachel to family friends—often pausing to smile and accept glasses of wine from men of all ages who are obviously hoping to intoxicate her into submission. Attention spills over onto Rachel; she's anxious from the overcrowding. Cerise also seems annoyed by the attention and pulls Rachel outside.

Cerise ducks around the side of the building and lights up a cigarette. "Watch for my mom—she'll kick my ass if she sees me smoking."

Rachel peeks back inside, spotting Cerise's mom deep in conversation, likely about the painting she keeps pointing at of two brown bears mounting a naked woman standing in the basket of a hot air balloon floating a few feet above the ground.

"Your dad's art is pretty sexual. Very…uh…avant-garde."

Cerise laughs and flicks ash. "You like it?"

"I don't think I've ever seen anything like it… Do you paint?"

Cerise breaks eye contact, glances down, and pulls her thin, dark-wool, knee-length jacket tighter. "I sketch a little."

"It's cool your dad is a professional artist."

Cerise beams. "He's actually my step-dad. That's why we all refer to him by name. My younger sister is his, but since my brother and I were already calling him Ryley they wanted to avoid confusion and keep us united."

"Ah."

"They're cousins, my parents." Cerise takes a step back, as

if expecting a reaction that will thwart any chance for long-term friendship.

Despite how jarring the comment initially seems, Rachel finds Cerise's candid honesty refreshing. "Jessie James, Edgar Allen Poe, Darwin, and Einstein were all married to their cousins."

"Are you serious?"

"Usually."

"Your turn." Cerise flicks the cigarette butt in the gutter and waits.

"...My grandfather had eight wives," she says—omitting the lack of blood relation.

"So, what do you have like two-hundred cousins!?"

"Good dating odds, I guess." Rachel winks.

Cerise looks up at the sky and laughs, linking arms with Rachel as they walk back inside. So many eyes are on them it's unnerving. Cerise generates enough energy to light up everyone else in the room. She's like a wayward star careening around the galaxy about to go supernova; men with an emotional death wish get in line for a turn to reprogram her GPS. But she has tunnel-vision for Rachel who can't remember anyone ever trying this hard to be her friend.

She hopes Cerise's interest won't burn out as fast as it ignited. Experience has taught Rachel that it's difficult to maintain long-term relationships. It may have been a product of her unstable childhood and transient nature. But she thinks it has more to do with social currency and what other people believe can be gained from being her friend. Her stripper friends want the employee discount at the porn shop. Guys want sex with a girl they hope is a freak in the sack.

The Light in the Sound

Sadie likes having a place to crash when she's drunk. Some people—the rare few—could care less about social currency and just want a good friend, and an even more select few, are willing to be a good friend back. Cerise seems like one of the rare few. Still, Rachel fears there's an ulterior motive beneath her beautifully broken exterior.

Quicksand

Rachel wakes from a recurring nightmare. Lying on her side, she can't see him standing beside the bed. Usually, she dreams in color, but this dream is always black and white and silent. She's a child, standing on a hill, looking down at her grandmother's house—a two-story colonial at the base of an adjacent hill—no other homes in sight. White lightning bolts from pale gray clouds in the night sky. The house is charred soot black, surrounded by a muddy, winding river. Wind bends slate-gray grass toward the house, as if pointing in the direction she should go. Rachel descends the hill. Her father is standing in the middle of the river, arms crossed with a solemn expression. He is wearing a white suit—reminiscent of the day she was baptized.

At eight years old, Rachel had dedicated her life to a deity carefully chosen from a selection of one. Still ignorant to the earthly expectations of men, barely able to spell the names of all her siblings, she *chose*—as her parents would say for years to come—a God to ensure her eternal salvation and was rewarded with cake and a new dress on a day other than her birthday.

A large dead tree growing from the bank, roots immersed in water, looms over her father. Crooked branches reach down, like long skinny fingers swirling the water around her feet and ankles. She takes a step back, but the slippery sandbank of the river, like quicksand, pulls her in and down. Water rushes up to her chest and tugs her below the frothy surface. Body parts—severed limbs—like logs rushing downstream, crash into her. Her father reaches in, lifting her above the carnage and rapids. She gasps for air. His mouth moves, but nothing comes out. He plunges her back into the water. She struggles to free herself from his grasp. Again, he lifts her out of the water, immediately thrusting her back into the murky depths. She wriggles free and swims toward the bank. Emily is standing at the edge—statuesque. Rachel reaches out to her, but she just stares off into the distance, then disappears.

Rachel grabs a tree limb, digging her nails into the soggy bark. Black blood oozes from her fingernails and runs down her arms. Slowly, she pulls herself out of the waves and collapses in the grass. She looks back; her father is gone. A younger man, taller and leaner, appears across the river. He scowls. She stands to run. He crosses the rapids with little effort, chasing her into the house. She hides in a dark closet. It's stale and warm and smells of old leather shoes. He bangs on the door, shaking the entire house. The closet shrinks until fear of suffocation forces her awake.

It takes a moment to catch her breath. Her chest feels heavy. She rolls over and sees him: the tall man with sunken cheeks and black iris' from her dream is standing beside her bed. She blinks. He doesn't disappear. Her heart races, and she croaks a muffled scream. He lunges at her. She rolls out of bed and scrambles down the hallway on her hands and knees into the living room, cramming her body into the small space between the couch and the wall near the front door.

A blinking street lamp casts wide stripes of burnt orange on the living room walls and carpet. She pulls her legs close to her chest. The room is cold. Her fingers are stiff. She exhales. Warm breath lingers in the cool air. Rocking back and forth, she squeezes her eyes shut so tight, tears stream down her face. An upholstery staple protruding from the side of the couch scrapes her shoulder. The living room slowly returns to its usual green glow from the DVD-player buttons.

She had dug her fingernails so deep into the palms of her hands it stings to relax her balled fists. A small bead of blood collected in the palm of her hand runs down her arm. Someone knocks on the door. Rachel freezes, wondering if she had screamed in her sleep again. Had someone heard? Sadie yells. Rachel jumps up and opens the door. Sadie scans Rachel, stopping on her bloody arm, "What the hell happened to you?" Sadie burps fruit juice and Tequila. Rachel shuts the door behind her, disappears down the hall and locks herself in the bathroom.

Sadie pounds on the door. "If you don't want me to puke on your carpet you better let me in."

"Jesus, Sadie— it's Tuesday night! What the hell are you drinking for?"

"I know, I know. I was out with Eric…You remember the guy from the other night?"

Rachel folds her arms and glares.

"I met his parents; his mom is a bartender—she just kept-em' comin'. I didn't want to be rude, of course—burp—but I can't go home. Can I pleeeeeease stay here tonight, Rach… Pleeeeeeeeease?"

"Like I'm gonna say no."

Sadie pinches Rachel's cheek. "I wuv you my little, choochie-chipmunk-cheeked friend."

Rachel is so relieved to have someone stay the night, she doesn't mind that Sadie doesn't really care about what happened to her.

"You have a hole in your shirt." Sadie pokes her finger into the hole. "I told you to stop doing Kung-Fu in your sleep." Stumbling down the hall, Sadie giggles. "Where the hell is all the food!?" she yells from the kitchen while Rachel is changing in the bedroom.

"I thought you were sick?"

"It comes in waves. Now I want Nachos!"

By the time Rachel finishes nuking a plate of tortilla chips, Sadie is passed out on the couch.

The Hanged Man

Five days after their date, Justin still hasn't returned Rachel's calls—except for the one missed call while she was asleep the morning after. For a while, going to work was easier than usual because she expected to see him, but each hopeful morning has resulted in a no-show. She hopes his absence from work is an indication that something other than trying to avoid her is going on. She thinks about calling Cerise and asking if she has any info on his whereabouts but decides it would make her look too desperate. She doesn't want to be *that* girl, so she maintains her normal routine in silent misery.

The shop never has more than one customer at a time, most of whom just want bottles of lube or a DVD from the clearance bin. Sadie calls three times, and Rachel finally answers on the last ring of the third call. Sadie rambles for twenty minutes, until Rachel says she has a customer and needs to go. Cerise calls. She presses Rachel for details because she doesn't *sound right*, but a shop vendor walks in, and this time Rachel really does have to go but promises to call back.

Steve Buckley, one of the shop DVD vendors, is a living cliché: trashy, fat-nosed, fast-talking, compulsive liar, and the only local pornographic filmmaker with a large following. Well, supposedly the only one who has something worth selling. Rachel dreads their bimonthly interactions when he brings in the new stock. Steve swaggers through the store with his typical cocksure manner. He picks up a piece of red-lace lingerie. Holding it up next to Rachel, he nods his head in approval, then eats a chocolate penis out of the counter display, throwing the wrapper on the floor. Running his hand through his dark, greasy hair, it clumps back to its original position. He pulls an invoice out of his jacket pocket and lays it on the counter. He always expects Rachel to pay cash and sign before he produces the merchandise. She finds the whole procedure obnoxious. Just being near him warrants a shower to wash away the slime his eyes leave on everything. She reminds herself she gets ten percent commission on top of the hourly pay.

"So, Rachel, honey, when you gonna do me a solid and be in one'a my flicks?"

"Keep dreamin'."

"Don't scoff, girly. I'm payin' my girls 4k a film these days, *plus* 1% off the top. And I know you can't top that plinkin' a cash-register all day." He makes beeping noises while pretending to push buttons on an invisible cash register.

"My self-respect isn't for sale this week—or *ever*, Steve-o."

"Everything's for sale! Wait 'til your perky, tan boobies become withered, saggy sunspots, then we'll see who's high-and-mighty!"

"Well, Steve, considering how old you are already, your dick should be shriveled, black, and about to fall off by then, so I'll always have the last laugh."

"Do you talk to your motha with that mouth, girly?"

"Do you?"

"Pssssht—episode seventeen, *Rest-home Rendezvous,* grandma number four—yeah, you guessed it—my mom's!"

"You're disgusting."

"Exactly why you want me."

Rachel scowls. She knows he's lying because last time he tried to convince her that his mom was a missionary in South Africa. And the time before that he claimed she was the head of a modeling agency. "Are we done?"

"Yeah, yeah, yeah. I'll see you in eight weeks. And a little tip…cleavage never killed nobody—think about it!"

Rachel flips him off as he walks out, then calls Cerise.

"My mom is having some of her astrology friends over tonight. I'm hoping you'll come by and hangout. But if you can't, I totally understand. I sent Justin a text earlier to make sure you two didn't already have—"

"Oh yeah, what did he say?" The stool tips and Rachel starts falling, catching herself on the counter just in time. Her chest tightens. If he answered Cerise's text and not hers, she knows he's avoiding her and that's that. It's over. She can't deal with the thought of Justin being a typical jerk who bails as soon as he gets laid.

"He hasn't responded."

Rachel is so relieved she almost falls anyway.

"So you wanna come tonight?"

"Sure."

"Yay!" Cerise yells into the phone and hangs up, texting the address and directions with an apology for hanging up so fast because she dropped the phone.

Rachel drives up to a two-story house. The yard is littered with pots filled with the dried, leafless stems of plants that never woke from hibernation. Wind chimes and faded windsocks hang from tree branches all over the yard. The gray picket fence bends toward a cracked sidewalk leading to the front door. A short porcelain dog in a tuxedo sits on the bottom stair holding a welcome sign.

A woman with curly gray hair wearing a colorful Mumu answers. A cloud of Nag-Champa incense floats out the doorway. The woman introduces herself as, Fernwren. She has four eyebrow piercings, two above each eye. However, she's not wearing the standard surgical-steel piercing jewelry Rachel is accustomed to seeing. Instead, her piercings hold four parakeet tail feathers—one yellow and one blue on each side. After working in a porn shop for so long, Rachel thought she'd seen it all, but is shocked by the small feathers sticking out of the woman's eyebrows and has a hard time hiding her surprise. Fortunately, Cerise's mom creates a distraction with introductions. Fernwren nibbles on crackers while three other women sitting on a stiff, puce-pink, Victorian couch in the middle of the living room scrutinize Rachel. No one else is quite as colorful as Fernwren, but they're certainly nothing like her stepmother's church group either.

Cerise's mom smiles warmly. "We just ran out of wine; we sent Cerise to the store. I hope you don't mind hanging out with just us old-ladies?"

"Speak for yourself," Beatrice, a youthful woman in a purple smock, says.

Fernwren cackles.

"We've already finished Astrology charts for the coming month, but Beatrice was just about to give Fernwren a Tarot reading. Would you like to go first?"

Rachel shrugs. "Sure." She's never had a Tarot reading. All she knows about Tarot cards, along with Ouija boards, Runes, and supposedly candles, is that they're used by Satan worshippers to summon demons—at least that's what her parents believe. Although, Rachel thinks her stepmother's disdain for candles has more to do with paranoia, governed by the same warped reasoning that somehow rationalizes tampons deflowering a woman, and has little to do with Satan. And none of these women look like they're intent is to reenact *The Exorcist.* Either way, Rachel is extremely curious about the Tarot.

Beatrice shuffles a deck of cards with colorful pastoral scenes and court-jester style characters in a myriad of poses. She selects what she refers to as a *significator card* intended to represent Rachel, and then asks her to cut the deck into three equal piles.

A thin layer of incense smoke blankets the room in an

evanescent veil. Rachel glances around. *No Devil yet—so far so good.*

Beatrice selects an even number of cards from each stack and lays out a cross configuration, mumbling as random cards appear. All the women gather round.

Rachel waits as everyone stares at the cards while bobbing their heads in unison, as if speaking to each other telepathically. "What?" she coaxes.

Beatrice resumes laying cards. Fernwren nods in approval and points to the spread, "You've got three queens already."

Beatrice flips over a card called *The Hanged Man*. It has a picture of a skinny man wearing green tights hanging upside down by one foot. "Do you sense things before they happen?" she asks.

"I suppose, maybe."

"No reason to hold back here, you're in good company," Cerise's mom says, handing Rachel a napkin and a cup of chamomile tea.

Beatrice frowns. An evil looking half-man, half-goat is on the next card. She grimaces as she reads D-E-A-T-H.

"No, no—no reason to be alarmed. The death card doesn't mean you're going to die. Oh, that would be just awful. It could mean someone you know has died or is going to die, but that is *extremely* rare. It usually just means something is troubling you or some bad news or even a bad experience is coming. No worries, though—it's a ways off—certainly isn't going to happen tomorrow." Beatrice pats Rachel's hand, then lays down the next card and continues frowning, "My my my."

"Jesus, Bee, stop scaring the poor girl." Cerise's mom shakes her head.

"Sorry. It's just that the next card indicates you're *not* prepared. Do you meditate, Rachel?" Beatrice asks.

"No."

All the women gasp in unison.

Cerise's mom runs over to a tall shelf covered in knick-knacks, mini-cacti, and disheveled book stacks. She pulls out a colorful book with swirls of light emanating from a female figure sitting cross-legged on the cover. "You should read this. Everything you ever need to know about meditation, chakras, and auras is in this book. It's all interrelated. The human body is like a giant battery. We give off an electromagnetic field of energy that creates an Aura. All living things have one. What's happening with your chakras can affect the strength of your Aura, so you always want them strong and active. Some people, like my Cerise, can see auras." She beams with pride.

The screen door slams and in walks Cerise, cheeks flushed from the cold. She glances down at the Tarot spread, "Uh oh."

"Oh shush!" Cerise's mom waves her arms, grabs the wine bottles, then disappears into the kitchen.

Cerise sits down next to Rachel. "Ooooooh looky here!" Cerise squeals like someone with a rattle trying to elicit a reaction from a baby. She points to a card with two people next to a river standing below a rainbow. "That means love is in your future!"

Rachel hopes it means Justin, but she can't help noticing that Cerise turns bright red as she rests her hand on Rachel's thigh.

Cerise's mom comes back from the kitchen and hands out glasses of wine—pauses, then grabs one of Cerise's breasts.

"I knew it!" she shrieks.

"What?" Cerise says defiantly.

"You're not wearing a bra again!"

"Come on, Mom! Why do you make such a big deal of it? You're the one who always lectures about being *all-natural*. Besides, I just read an article about bras restricting growth, and I really think there's something to it."

"Your boobs are big enough!" Cerise's mom looks at Rachel. "Will you please tell her they're fabulous!"

Rachel squirms. Her family rarely hugs. They certainly never grab each other's breasts or have conversations about them.

"Fine!" Cerise's mom throws her hands in the air. "You'll have big boobs all right—you'll have giant bananas hanging down to your waist, then we'll see how you feel about a bra!"

"Oh, let the girl be. I haven't worn a bra since I was twenty-five, and I don't see the problem," Fernwren says.

The room falls silent. Everyone gawks at Fernwren's enormous breasts nearly touching her knees.

Cerise explodes into laughter, and everyone chimes in.

"My turn!" Fernwren says, attempting to squelch the laughter. The room settles. "It's my turn for a reading, Bee—I need to know what to do about the sale of my house." Cerise grabs Rachel's arm, dragging her upstairs as the group rattles on about subprime mortgages and high interest rates.

Cerise's pink room is barren. "Ignore the echo," she says. "I moved out for a couple years and lived on my own until a few months ago. I'm just crashing here until I find a new place."

Cerise pulls her shirt over her head, tosses it on the floor, and leans down to thumb through a box of clothes. Her round breasts are like ripe cannonball gourds on a vine: ready for picking. Rachel feels like a high school student in an awkward locker room moment and flounders for conversation. She looks down and pretends to be interested in a magazine lying next to the bed. Cerise picks up a red bra and lingers—obviously waiting for a reaction.

Rachel spits out the first thing that comes to mind, "I agree with your mom, your boobs are fabulous."

Cerise beams while putting on the bra. "Hey—you want a shot? I've got a bottle of Patron stashed somewhere." She rummages and pulls a bottle with a couple inches of tequila out from behind the television then does a silly dance. Rachel doesn't feel like drinking, but Cerise is so excited she doesn't want to disappoint her. Cerise pours two double-shots into Care Bear Dixie cups, gulps one with ease and refills, then passes Rachel hers. "Toast! To new friends and great tits."

"Cheers!" Rachel lightly taps Cerise's Love-a-lot Bear with her Tenderheart Bear, choking on the slow burn of warm tequila.

"You wanna see some pictures?" Cerise pulls out a stack of family photos from the early eighties. Most are of her as a toddler covered in finger paint, wearing nothing but ruffled panties.

Rachel is jealous. She'd never seen any pictures of herself when she was that young. They'd supposedly been lost in one of the family moves. But she wouldn't be shocked to find out her stepmother had thrown them out during one of her many fits of jealous rage over Rachel's dad doting on her as a little girl. Eventually, the tantrums won, and Rachel barely ever spoke to her father for anything other than arguments over using words like fabulist and ephebophilia in reference to the founder of their church.

"Check this one out." Cerise hands Rachel a faded picture of a muscular blond guy standing next to a surfboard. "That's Ryley when he was in high school—isn't he hot!?"

"Yeah...sure."

She kisses the photo and places it on her bedside table apart from the rest of the stack. Rachel can't imagine thinking any picture of her own dad is that attractive, but Cerise's family is closer and more liberal with their sexuality, so she decides not to be weirded out.

"I wish I could find a guy like my dad. Guys are just dickheads these days. I think I may give up on guys all together—how about you?"

"Justin seems nice."

"He's cool. He doesn't seem like the relationship type, though. Don't misunderstand—I think you two are adorable together. I'm just yet to see him commit to anyone. But who knows, maybe I'm wrong and he's just waiting for someone like you—what do I know?"

But Justin hasn't called in so long, Rachel can't help thinking that Cerise might be right.

Brass Knuckles

Rachel arrives home at a quarter to midnight. Someone had parked a black Dodge Omni in her designated space, so she reluctantly parks in the only available space on the dark side of the building. She kicks the Omni's front tire a few times, hoping to set off an alarm to get the owner's attention, but nothing happens. She leaves a note on the windshield.

The shadow of someone standing around the corner stretches onto the adjacent sidewalk. She assumes it's a neighbor but sets three keys to stick out between her fingers when balled up in a fist to spike her punch if any psychos are hiding in the bushes.

She rounds the corner, and the person attached to the shadow jumps back. Rachel drops her purse and throws her fists in the air.

Justin throws his hands up in surrender. "Whoa,

Wolverine—take a deep breath!"

"Holy Shit! What are you doing here? And where the hell have you been?"

Justin looks suddenly somber.

She opens the door and directs him to the couch, then feeds Ewoka who's hot on her heels. The apartment still smells like the chicken burrito she'd nuked for dinner the night before. She lights a mulberry candle. "This better be good—I'm expecting an alien abduction or a coma," she says with a smile.

"Do I earn any points waiting outside for two hours until you got home?"

She sits down next to him.

"I almost called a couple of times, but I didn't want to dump my shit on you, so I decided to wait until I sorted some stuff out. It's just been a really rough week."

"Sheesh—did someone die?"

"My dad wrecked my truck on the way home from the bar last Saturday. I never would have let him take it if I'd known that's where he was going. He just got his license back. It was revoked for a year, so I guess I thought, maybe—fuck, I don't know what I thought."

"It's not your fault. If we're not allowed to blame our parents for the shit we pull, we sure as hell shouldn't take the blame for theirs."

Justin smiles.

"Is he okay?"

"He broke both his legs. And I thought my truck was insured under my parents' policy because they said it would get me a better rate. But it turns out the money I gave them every month for insurance was actually going toward the stock of Budweiser longnecks in the garage, so now *I have to pay* for the repairs. I can't even drive it. I had to borrow my sister's car just to come over here."

Rachel can't think of anything consoling to say that won't sound trite, so she puts her hand on his knee.

He shakes his head. "I'm sorry for not calling, then dumping all this on you. I was afraid if I waited any longer you might not speak to me again, and I didn't want you to think I was avoiding you."

"I get reclusive when stuff like this happens, too."

"Really? Is your dad a drunk?"

"Might as well be, he's just as violent and erratic, but no. I think you're winning the shittiest parent award right now."

Justin sinks lower into the couch.

"How long do you have your sister's car?"

"I'm good for the night. I dropped her at a friend's house. But you're probably tired and have to work tomorrow, so I won't keep you up. I just wanted to tell you in person what's been going on."

"I don't work until later tomorrow. You could crash here tonight if you want."

"Seriously, that would be great. Dad's in a wheelchair, running into everything and throwing shit all over the house, and mom is threatening to go back to Mexico to live with grandma."

"Your mom is Hispanic?" Rachel never noticed before, but his large, black-brown eyes and olive complexion made sense. Still, she never would have guessed he was anything other than Caucasian.

"I get that a lot. My dad's family migrated from Russia. He grew up in Texas and met my mom one summer on a beach in Mexico while he was on leave from the military. I'm just a super-mutt."

"Interesting."

"It wasn't very interesting when people keyed *spic* in the side of my car in high school and filled my mailbox with Taco Shack coupons. But compared to what the kids who actually looked Mexican went through, I can't complain. I guess it's just the downside of growing up in a predominantly white neighborhood."

"I don't remember you being picked on?"

"I didn't have much trouble before high school, but I didn't know very many people then, either."

"I would have been your friend."

Justin smiles and leans forward. "Hopefully, we would have been more than friends."

She feels like an egg of Silly Putty whenever he gets that close. The moment she makes contact with his cola-flavored tongue, the week of agony spent speculating about where he was and why he hadn't called, vanishes.

He pulls back. "Have you been drinking?" He looks worried, like she might have been out on a date with another guy.

She hesitates. She hadn't even drunk enough to get drunk. "I was at Cerise's house—"

"Just saying *Cerise* would have sufficed."

"That bad, huh?"

"I'm surprised you're getting along so well."

"Yeah, I don't usually get along so well with other girls."

"Just don't let her mess with your head. She has a tendency to play games—at least she did with Ian. Who knows, maybe she's different with chicks. Just watch your back. Something about her has always made me wary."

"Do I need to change my number?"

He smiles. "It's not like she's gonna pop out from under your bed and suck your soul through a crazy straw. I'm just saying she likes to make up little stories to get her way. Plus, she's a lush."

He sounds exactly like what he is: the friend of a guy who dated someone going through a hard time. His opinions are biased, but nonetheless valid. She can corroborate his uneasy feeling with her own, but she has a sympathetic theory for the motivation behind Cerise's erratic behavior and doesn't think she's in any kind of danger. Either way, she has no intention of being her next victim or allowing Justin to endure the fallout. But Cerise is the least of her worries while she has Justin's attention.

Crash into Me

Justin is preparing to leave. Rachel peeks at him with one eye open. He folds the flannel, Pink Panther pajama pants and oversized, Dave Matthews Band t-shirt he'd borrowed, stacking them at the bottom of the bed, then shoves his keys and wallet in his pocket. "Sorry," he whispers, as he leans over the side of the bed and kisses her, "I was trying not to wake you."

Rachel yawns. "I have to get up anyway." She's relieved she made it through the night without waking up, or *half-waking up*.

Justin stands at the end of the bed. "My mom wants to know if you can come to dinner tomorrow."

"Sure," Rachel says casually, not wanting to let on that she's aware of what meeting his parents implies.

"Really—that's cool with you?" Justin is less discreet as

he gathers the rest of his things. Slipping a note under her pillow, he tugs on her earlobe and promises to call later.

Ewoka jumps on the bed and nuzzles Rachel's arm. She cuddles the ball of calico fur and thinks about Justin. He had asked so many questions about her that she felt naked before he even started exploring her body, for what then seemed like hours. He had kissed every curve and freckle from her forehead to her toes. He's a giver in bed. They were like two marshmallows on warm pavement all night. She felt an invigorating infusion of his energy. And for the first time, she knows what it's like to make love. Before Justin, she scoffed at the term *making love*. It seemed like a matronly way to describe sex, too proper for it to be any good. Passionate, sweaty, quick, and sometimes even painful sex is invigorating, and guys respond well to it—always coming back for more; some even obsessively—mirroring the relationships that come with it, but Justin obviously isn't interested in that. He has bigger plans for Rachel; she can feel it in the way he holds the back of her head and kisses her deep during every orgasm. She hiccups now thinking about it and denies the slow-growing awareness that she may be falling in love. Her only regret is that their first time was tainted by her emotional baggage.

She pulls the note out from under the pillow, holding her breath while reading:

> *Hey, jerkoff! You're not paying for this parking spot—I am! Park here again and you'll get towed!*

Justin's reply:

> *Simmer down, toughie-tough girl. Hopefully, last night was worth losing a parking space.*
> *(smiley face)*

She laughs. The phone rings twice. Her stepmother's voice
is an unwelcome surprise—spiritless with a nearly inaudible
lisp (more pronounced when she's tired or frustrated). Only a
few moments into the conversation, Rachel feels like she fell
off of the retaining wall into the polar bear exhibit at the zoo.

"Your cousin Hannah died," her stepmother says, not
likely upset by the death, rather annoyed by having to call.

"What happened?"

"She was driving on the freeway with her friends, and
there was a bee in the car."

"That's awful."

"She shouldn't have been on the freeway, and she shouldn't
have had friends in the car."

"Why didn't the Holy Ghost protect her—was she
drinking caffeinated beverages again?"

"You can't blame God for something so tragic!"

"If she had survived, you'd all be thanking him."

"I don't have time for this. If I wanted to be chastised for
my beliefs I'd call Emily."

Rachel's stepmother came into her life two years after
Emily left Rachel's father for what was supposed to be a ten-
month teaching job in South America that had turned into
two years and divorce papers. Despite choosing not to play
the wife and mother role anymore—or at least that was the
story told to Rachel—Emily hated her replacement. Rachel
never saw anyone stand up to her stepmother the way
Emily did. Rachel loved the show and Emily knew it. One
of Rachel's most satisfying memories is of the day Emily
came for a surprise visit and pulled Rachel out of school to
go shopping, causing her stepmother to go berserk. Rachel's

father had to take the day off from work to keep the women from killing each other. Emily was deeply bothered by Rachel's stepmother's *fanatical ways* (her words) and felt that she'd brainwashed Rachel's father with her *holier-than-thou bullshit*. No one crafted offensive language quite like Emily. She gave every expletive emphasis to burrow and fester as deep as possible below Rachel's stepmother's skin. Like a big-breasted model with glossy red lips and sculpted barrel bangs holding a cancer stick on a billboard, Emily made words—Rachel would get her mouth peppered for even thinking—seem bewitching.

It was forbidden to talk about her. Any mention of Emily made her stepmother livid. Just saying her name resulted in an angry grimace, a slap on the wrist, and subsequent silence for the rest of the day. Rachel is shocked to hear her stepmother mention Emily now.

"Have you heard anything?" her stepmother asks.

In December, Rachel had received a photo of a rainbow and a couple of holiday postcards from Puerto Limón on the Caribbean shore of Costa Rica, but she hasn't heard from her in a few months—a bit longer than usual.

"Anyway, I just called to tell you about Hannah, since you *used* to be friends with her."

Loss of Hannah's friendship was part of the fallout for Rachel leaving their religion, and she hasn't spoken to her in nearly eight years, but not for lack of trying. She suspects that part of her stepmother's motivation for promptly reporting Hannah's death is to make Rachel feel guilty for turning her back on their God and subsequently Hannah. But it's just a reminder that their religion advocates disloyalty to friends and family in exchange for eternal salvation. After of course, giving ten percent of their income to ensure the pearly gates are open upon arrival. She's saddened that Hannah spent her life being lied to about where she was really going after her car crossed three lanes and she was thrown through her open window into oncoming traffic. But she's more upset by losing her friend for the second time. And this time it's not buffered by hope for eventual reconciliation, but she'll never reveal her grief to her stepmother who will misconstrue it as guilt.

"How is everyone else doing?"

"Fine." She rarely—if ever, informs Rachel of her three half-siblings (one sister and two brothers) status. On the rare occasion that Rachel is permitted to speak to anyone, her stepmother hovers over the timed conversation, fearful that Rachel will "infect" them with independent or dissident thoughts.

If Rachel had known what was going to come out of her stepmother's mouth next, she would have faked a dying battery and hung up. Instead, she struggles to keep it together as her stepmother says, "Your dad's going to be in Seattle for a sales conference in a couple of weeks and he wants to visit you, or *whatever.*"

Or whatever, plays back in Rachel's mind. Ending on *visit* wouldn't have stressed the point. Not the real point, at least. The point that putting the effort forth for any kind of meeting is a strain she wants acknowledged. Probably hoping Rachel will back out so she can feign the role of the rejected, suffering parent while crying to her extended family at the next holiday BBQ about how Rachel never appreciates their efforts to reach out to her.

Rachel takes a deep breath. Play it cool, she tells herself. He may never come. Wouldn't be the first time they played this game. "Cool, *whatever*—just have him call me when he's in town."

Her stepmother mumbles as if writing down a phone message. "So how are you doing?" Her voice trails.

"I'm dating someone new."

"How's that going?" Her full attention is back on Rachel.

She hears the barely audible cue in her stepmother's voice. Something that couldn't be so easily detected by someone who doesn't know her well, but Rachel catches it. The sound stems from recognition that she might have an opportunity to gather information she can use against her in the future, but Rachel won't play that game. She knows better, and plans to keep any details to herself, except the one tidbit she knows will aggravate her stepmother and further solidify her dissent from their way of thinking.

"His mom invited me to dinner."

"Really. What is she like?" There's another cue, but this time Rachel's playing along with a purpose.

"We haven't met yet, but I know she's from Mexico."

"Mexico! Are they Hispanic?" Disdain is thick in her enunciations.

"His mother is."

"I have a bad feeling about this boy."

"Of course, you do."

"Don't try and peg me a racist. It has nothing to do with that. I'm just concerned about the cultural differences in the way *they* think and raise a family."

"Of course."

"Think whatever you want, but intuition tells me this relationship will be a disaster."

"Whatever."

Rachel's stepmother doesn't have an intuitive bone in her body. And Rachel knows damn well that her parents are racist from the jokes they tell and discomfort they exhibited when she had brought home ethnic friends from school. Their religion even taught that dark skin was a curse, until doctrine was changed because it threatened to revoke their tax-free status. But when Rachel dated men of various races, she found a bunch of average, American men with great complexions. None of whom dissented notably from the core family values of any white-guy she'd ever known. Of course, rebellion isn't her motivation for dating Justin, but it's definitely a perk.

"Be careful."

Rachel mockingly agrees, tired of arguing with someone with so little interest in playing more than a minor role in her life via a few short telephone conversations each year. Rachel can never tell whether her stepmother feels defeated, abandoned, inferior, or superior. It's probably more than just one, but no mood ever presents opportunity for reconciliation; mutual tolerance is the best they ever arrive at. And this is better than her relationship with her father. He's built a reputation in sales as being able to sell bikinis to Eskimos, so she assumes he considers it one of his greatest failures that he could never sell her their God.

"I'm late for work," Rachel says, quickly ending the miserable conversation before it gets any worse. Still, she's lonely and wishes for someone she could *really* confide in about Justin. She almost calls Sadie, but changes her mind, remembering how those conversations always go, which is an abrupt redirection to Sadie's issues. It could also result in Sadie wanting to hookup with Justin. It isn't that she sluttishly targets the guys Rachel likes; it's more of an insecure need to be the most desirable girl in the room. But she often falls flat when competing with Rachel, unless the guy is just looking for sex, then Sadie wins, and Rachel is relieved. But she knows Justin would be annoyed by Sadie's antics and she doesn't want to watch her suffer.

Without thinking, she dials the last known number she had for Emily. No longer in service.

Rachel arrives at work ten minutes late because of her stepmother's phone call. She tries to tamper with the clock that punches time cards, but she doesn't have the proper tools to remove the cover. Instead, she opts not to punch-in at all and plea forgetfulness, rather than endure the write-up they'll put in her performance file for being late three times that month.

The large display window projects wide beams of bright mid-morning sun on sparkly, pink and green jelly dildos and rainbow feather boas. The shop is a lascivious carnival of color; it seems almost kid-friendly—almost. The district manager had left a message on the machine informing Rachel that Neeka quit, so she's on her own this coming week. Rachel isn't shocked. The turnover rate is high. Even though Rachel has stuck it out, she envies Neeka, and hopes her own days at the porn shop are limited. But she still hasn't found an alternative that will pay enough to survive on her own.

She tries to reconnect with the part of herself that used to be excited to work there because it's sexy, edgy, and defiant. She initially bought into the "empowering" speeches and gained confidence in her own sexuality, but it didn't define her. Unlike the rare few who have been there as long or longer and are completely content. Being comfortable in that environment is such a small part of her personality, she has to compartmentalize the more complex aspects of herself just to get through the day, and she always feels out of sync. She respects the girls who let it define their identity. For some, it isn't just a job, it's a career, and they hope to eventually get into porn or franchise their own shop. But that isn't Rachel. She hates to think she's better, because that would denigrate women she respects, but she knows she's destined for something different, something more meaningful—to her at least. Something she can wake up in the morning and be proud of, and she knows she has to do it before the longing takes a toll on her. Like a prostitute pulled off the street and ripped out of her black leather mini skirt, then shoved into an eggshell-white wedding dress with a fancy hair twist, one might never know where she'd come from and how long it had taken her to get there. Most people only see what's standing right in front of them, but the prostitute is always aware of what's hiding beneath the shiny dress. And Rachel doesn't want to become dulled to the beauty in the world, the way constantly interacting with so much ugly will inevitably make her.

A short, brown-haired girl walks in. She has long hair pulled back in a ponytail that brushes her ass when it sways.

She smiles at Rachel and looks her up and down, staring for an uncomfortably long time. Rachel assumes she's bisexual or a lesbian stripper—the shop's best customers, rivaled only by sex-deprived homemakers shopping for things that buzz quietly in the bathtub. She picks up a flesh-colored object shaped like a small Christmas tree—about the size of her forearm.

"What's this?"

"An anal plug," Rachel says. She's asked that question at least two or three times per day and is convinced they're required to display it for that fact alone. During the two years she's worked there, she's never sold even one, and assumes it's intended to open a dialogue with the customers to up-sell other merchandise.

The girl quickly, and carefully, places it back on the shelf, then wipes her hand on her jeans. This is also a typical reaction that makes Rachel shake her head because if it *had* been used, she would want a hell of a lot more than a quick wipe on her jeans.

"Can I help you find anything?"

"Just looking, but thanks." The girl turns and shoots Rachel an intense smile, filled with expectation—way over the top, borderline creepy.

"Have we met?" Rachel asks, hoping not to offend someone she's expected to know.

"Definitely not." The girl picks up a hard-plastic, orange vibrator in a box and shakes it, like a kid in a toy store looking for things that giggle or talk, then tries to take it out of the package.

"No worries, we test all battery-operated items before

they leave the store due to the *no-returns policy.*"

The girl puts the vibrator down and glances back at the anal-plug with an obvious sense of relief. "So, do you *like* working here?"

"It's a fun place to hangout. Why—are you looking for a job?"

The girl laughs. "My mom would kill me." Then she zeroes in on Rachel's favorite, shiny, red-latex, knee-high boots. "Oh damn, those are fabulous!" She pulls a boot off the shelf and looks like she's about to start licking it. "I'm a size seven," she says.

Rachel disappears into the back to search for the size and returns to find the girl shoeless, feet wagging in anticipation.

The girl pulls the boots on, zips them up to her knees, and marches around the shop with her pants rolled up to her thighs.

"They look great on you," Rachel says honestly—though the prospect of a three-hundred-dollar sale would have justified a lie. Rachel listens to the girl rationalizing the expenditure in every drawn out *ohhhh* as she turns to view them in all possible angles. The longer she keeps the boots on, the closer Rachel comes to closing the sale, so she waits patiently. All the while touting how versatile they would be with a number of different outfits.

The girl finally sits down, slips them off, then holds them up like a prized trophy and sighs. "My brother will kill me if I come home with a pair of stripper boots."

"The last thing that will get us laid is letting our brothers dress us."

The girl nods in agreement and perks back up. "I do need

something big enough to sneak that orange vibrator into the house."

Rachel smiles.

"What the hell—Justin can kiss my ass."

Rachel freezes while pulling black tissue paper out of the shoebox. "Justin?" Relaxing as she remembers how common that name is, and how ridiculous it is to think the girl might be referring to *her* Justin. "Is that your brother?"

The girl stares intently waiting for a reaction.

Rachel gulps.

"You're, Rachel, right?"

Double gulp. "Yep."

"I thought so—you're dating my brother."

Rachel glances out the window at the black Dodge Omni she'd left the note on the windshield of last night—now parked in front of the shop—and wonders how she hadn't noticed it sitting there this entire time.

The girl holds out her hand. "I'm Tanzi—it's nice to meet you. He said to leave you alone until I met you at dinner tomorrow, but I thought this would be way more fun."

"Way more fun," Rachel says—a nervous laugh follows.

"And with all of the family drama, my mom's a real beast lately, so it will be a miracle if I'm even at dinner, but I really wanted to meet you. Anyway, I need to get back to work, but I *have* to have those boots."

Tanzi grabs the orange vibrator and a handful of grape-flavored condoms. "I assume this transaction will be confidential," she says with an exaggerated wink.

Rachel smiles, throws a free handful of penis chocolates in the bag and wishes Tanzi luck sneaking it all into the house.

"That's half the fun." She giggles and turns to leave. "See you tomorrow!...Maybe!...Nice meeting you!"

Rachel plops down on the stool behind the counter. *Justin is going to kill me.*

Another White Dash

achel arrives at Justin's parents' house near dusk. The porch light casts a semi-circle of light across the freshly cut lawn. What used to be his flawless, shiny blue truck is parked next to a tattered basketball hoop alongside the driveway. The concave frontend advertises the recent tragedy, and a stray cat has taken refuge under the immovable heap. Rachel feels partially to blame. The four orgasms she had on his lap in the front seat (just one day before the accident) undoubtedly saturated the truck with her energy—an energy that often feels cursed by the negativity that surrounds her. Justin sneaks up and pinches her sides. She jumps. "Holy Bujesus!"

He laughs. "What's with lingering outside—you avoiding my family?"

"Maybe." She smiles shyly.

"They're gonna love you—just ignore my dad. The pain-pills make him more crazy than usual, but he'll probably just stay in the TV room and ignore everyone anyway."

He kisses her gently and her nerves relax. Until she walks through the front door and his mother barrels toward her waiving a spatula.

"It's so wonderful to meet you, Rachel," his mother says. She's short with dark skin and a square face. She looks more Navajo than Hispanic, but Rachel can hear Mexico in the way she dances with her R's. Her name never sounded lovelier than when it rolled out of his mother's mouth. She throws her arms around Rachel and smothers her face in black, spicy hair, then grabs Rachel's shoulders and pushes her away. "My God, if you were a foot shorter, you and my Tanzi could be sisters! I don't know if I like the idea of you dating your sister's twin, Justin. That's very Fraudian." She winks at Rachel.

"Freudian, Mom—it's Freudian."

"Don't correct your mother in front of company—that's rude."

Justin rolls his eyes and shrugs.

"Sit down, Rachel. Tell me why you're worthy of stealing my son."

"Mom, come on!"

"Kidding, kidding—just joking—take a chill pill!" She waves at Justin dismissively. Patting a couch cushion with a large tangerine floral print, she beckons Rachel to sit. "I can already see why you like her so much. She has a beautiful face, like a flower, and wide hips. If I had hips like that my babies wouldn't have been born with pointy little pin heads."

Justin sits down on the couch next to Rachel and shakes his head.

"Where do you work, Rachel?"

She opens her mouth to respond—

"In a clothing store near the camera shop," Justin says.

"Let the girl speak for herself, Justin—jeez." I'm so sorry my son has no manners."

Rachel laughs nervously. After meeting his sister and hearing their mother's opinion of the porn shop, she'd planned to lie, but is frustrated about not being given the chance to decide. "It's pretty boring, just clothes—oh, and scarves."

"Scarves! I love scarves!" His mother's enthusiasm is exaggerated. "My younger sister Ramona and I used to knit scarves and sell them on the side of the road to earn money for candy and grain for our sheep."

"Sheep?" Rachel asks.

"Mom was raised on a farm."

Justin's mother throws her arms in the air. "And there he goes again—as if we women don't have voices of our own—you're too much like your father!" She points her finger, as if scolding a small child.

Justin looks wounded.

"Do you believe in Jesus, Rachel?" she asks.

"Yes," Rachel says after a moment of hesitation. She thinks that 2,000 years ago a man named Jesus preached a theology he plagiarized from Eastern philosophies that originated long before his time. Rachel doesn't believe Jesus was who he believed he was—or just who his disciples claimed he was, but she thinks it's very likely that he was a real person. She just hopes his mother won't press for specifics on her *belief.*

"Wonderful! Who wants tacos?" His mother jumps out of the chair with such force it bounces backward and nearly knocks over a plant on a small wood stand. "Lewis—Joel—dinner!" She ushers Justin and Rachel to a wood-laminate table, somehow preserved since the 70's. Rachel sits down on a high back, wrought iron chair with a bright red cushion wrapped in plastic.

"Damn it, Marita—I told you I wasn't hungry. Just bring me another beer!" A man with a bald pointy skull grunts between short breaths as he wheels himself down the hallway. He has a cast on each leg but is obviously quite tall. Even in a wheelchair, he is nearly as tall as Justin's mother is while standing.

"You're eating with the family tonight, Lewis. We have company—Justin's friend, Rachel, is here."

He looks directly at Rachel. He has a flushed, blotchy-red face, piss-yellow eyes, and smells of stale cigarette. "Who the hell are you?" he asks.

"For God's sake, Lewis, I just told you she's Justin's friend. Don't be so rude!" His mother shakes her head.

"What the hell is burning?" Lewis yells.

"Nothing! Go to the table. Joel—dinner!" Justin's mom zips around the kitchen trying to get everything on the table as fast as possible.

"Can I help with anything?" Rachel asks.

"Of course not, you're our guest," Marita says.

"Yeah—get me a Longneck," Lewis says.

"Come on, Dad, take it down a notch." Justin signals Rachel to stay put as he stands to fetch the beer.

"Don't tell me what to do in my own house!" Lewis flings

his arm out, knocking over the open ketchup bottle. Globs of red goop spill into Rachel's lap.

Marita races across the room with a towel. "Oh Lord, I'm so sorry, Rachel.... Dammit, Lewis—just drink your beer and shut up!"

Justin turns red and balls his fists.

"It's okay, everyone just calm down. It will rinse right out." She points Rachel toward the bathroom and squeezes Justin's shoulder, tells him to take a deep breath, then wheels Lewis and his beer down the hallway back into the TV room.

Rachel spends a few extra minutes collecting herself in the bathroom. A sun-washed painting of the Virgin Mary hangs across from the toilet. Rachel wonders how many times Marita had pled with the nearly faceless image for strength. She pulls her shirt down as far as possible in a failed attempt to cover the faded-orange ketchup stain that looks like her period leaked through her jeans.

Justin, his mom, Tanzi, and an older, less attractive version of Justin—with long, stringy blond hair, are all sitting at the table waiting. Justin introduces the butt-rock doppelganger as his brother, Joel, who is busy biting a cherry tomato in half in a feeble attempt to squirt Tanzi. Tomato juice and drool dribble down his sleeveless, Metallica t-shirt. He looks up to greet Rachel with a tomato seed stuck to his chin.

"What's up," Joel says, never raising his eyes above Rachel's chest.

"Nice to meet you," Rachel responds.

"Obviously! You ragged all over yourself." Joel snort-laughs.

"You're a dick," Justin says.

"Whatever—she's here—can I fucking eat now?"

Marita smacks the back of Joel's head. "Not at the table."

"My brother is a pig, but it's nice to meet you." Tanzi winks and reaches to shake Rachel's hand.

Rachel wonders if Justin was adopted.

Marita stabs at chunks of lettuce. Her fork scrapes the porcelain plate causing a disconcerting screech. Rachel imagines her picturing her husband and son's face on the plate. "I'm very sorry for my family's horrible behavior tonight. It's not usually like this."

Tanzi coughs up some water. "Yeah right," she gurgles.

Marita shoots Tanzi a *shut up* look. "So, what do you two kids have planned tonight?" she asks with a strained smile.

"Movie," Justin says. This is news to Rachel, but she catches on when he nudges her leg under the table.

"That's nice. What are you going to see?"

"A romantic comedy," Rachel says, giving Justin a *you owe me* look.

Joel makes a loud, wet, fart-like noise with his mouth.

"What are *you* doing tonight, Joel—sitting in your room masturbating?" Justin says.

Joel opens his mouth full of chewed taco shell and olives.

Marita mumbles something in Spanish. Her fork scrapes the plate so hard this time Rachel wonders if she's going to choke on glaze. "For God's sake, Justin."

"Sorry, Mom."

"So will you be back tonight?"

"I'm staying at Rachel's."

"Yeah, and I'm crashing at Anna's house tonight," Tanzi says.

This time Rachel thinks Marita's fork chips the plate. Dinner ends in silence.

"I am so sorry," Justin says, sliding into the passenger seat in Rachel's car. The headlights reflect off the eyes of the cat hiding in the shadows beneath his crumpled truck. They sit in the driveway for a moment watching the two glowing balls hover a few inches above the ground.

Justin looks embarrassed. "I was really hoping they'd be on best behavior."

"I thought your mom and sister were really nice."

"I should have prepped you better to meet my Dad and douche-bag brother."

"How—by making me drink a six-pack while listening to the Mötley Crüe discography? I'll pass."

Justin laughs.

"Just wait until you meet *my* family!" She smiles and kisses him. He didn't mention spending the night at her place before dinner, but she's pleased that he is. His family is dramatically different from hers, yet they create the same type of conflict-ridden, negative energy she grew up in and she wants to take him as far away as possible. She wants to be the rainbow in his cloud.

She blasts the radio and watches the broken lines on the road run into each other. Justin is silent for most of the ride to the theater. They skip concessions and he seems disinterested in even holding her hand during the movie.

Back at the apartment, their motions imitate the night before. Justin borrows pajamas, but this time he doesn't do a silly dance and make a scene of wearing her clothes. Sex is robotic. Even though he seems satisfied, it leaves her wondering if that's what intercourse with the same person for twenty-years might feel like. She suspects it's worse because she doesn't have twenty years of good memories to buffer the bad night, which leaves her feeling hollow and more alone than she might if he weren't even there.

Sadie had called twice during the movie. Rachel considers slipping out of bed and calling her back to escape the tension, but she's afraid leaving will just create more tension. Instead, she labors to fall asleep while Ewoka thumps around the living room.

Why So Sarah

Morning brings no reprieve. Justin is silent and distant. She wants to grab him, shake him, and say, *fuck it—it doesn't matter—screw those assholes! You can move in with me and borrow my car whenever you need.* Instead, she toasts bagels while he showers.

She stands in front of the small kitchen window, looking out on the gray day. Long raindrops plink the glass, cutting rivers through valleys of sprinkles. Drizzle paints a dark shadow on the sidewalk below. Slowly, it fills the space between each crack in the chalky cement sections, eventually reaching the grassy edge.

Justin's phone chimes. Convincing herself it's Kaleb or Ian, she tries to ignore it. The fifth chime exhausts her willpower. Just as she's about to reach for the phone, he walks out of the bathroom and sits down in front of his cold bagel.

"Thanks," he says through cream cheese lips.

She smiles.

He eats half a bagel while reading the messages. Finishing in silence, he swipes a glob of cream cheese off the plate and sucks it off his finger. "I want to talk to you about something." His tone is cold and distant. He stares out the window as if plotting an escape route. "I've got a lot of shit to deal with right now, and I'm gonna have to pick up more shifts to afford my truck repairs, and I don't want to weigh you down with titles so you feel some sort of obligation or whatever...Uh, I guess what I'm trying to say is...I don't think I'm good boyfriend material right now."

He struck down titles that were never established, setting them back further than if he had said nothing. She had never pressured him for a commitment. The audacity that he would contrive a conversation based on the mere possibility of expectation is especially off-putting. She gulps down large lumps of air and sits in silence, afraid of crying if she takes a breath to speak.

"Don't get me wrong. I don't want to stop seeing each other. I just don't want you to feel like we have to be exclusive. I think we should keep it casual and be open to see other people."

"I thought you're too busy to date?"

"I just mean you. I don't want to make you wait around for me to find time for us."

"Well, it's really *thoughtful* of you to decide *for me* what I should or shouldn't commit to this, but I don't work like that."

"I thought after meeting my family you'd understand. I was going to move out after graduation, but now that's fucked up because of my damn truck. Can't you just give me some time to sort some shit out? I really like you and I really like us, but I don't know how much I can be there for you right now."

The low rumble of passing thunder sends Ewoka scampering out from under the kitchen table. She slides across the white linoleum floor, hops onto the couch, then buries herself beneath a blanket creating a small round lump sticking out of the middle cushion. Rachel wants to climb inside with her. Determined not to expose how much emotion she's already invested in the prospect of the relationship he's ending before it even started, she takes a deep breath and speaks slowly, "I'm just not the type of person to abandon someone when it gets a little rough."

"Come on—don't label me as *that guy.*"

"*But*, I get it. I've been there. I understand the whole emotionally-exhausted-and-don't-know-how-much-you-have-to-give thing. I just can't be the girl who thinks something good is on hold because you need to work some shit out, and then run into you with a big-breasted blonde at a bar and end up feeling like an idiot for having an emotional response because *I* agreed to be non-exclusive."

He shifts in the chair. "I'm not playing you like that."

"The possibility of it doesn't work for me. I'm not demanding. I understand if you're too busy to call every night or go out some weekends. But gawd—you have to at least give me the chance to show you what I'm like before you *assume* I'm gonna be too clingy to deal with while you glue your life back together."

"I don't think you're cling— "

"Well, I'm not a sit-on-the-sideline-and-cheer-for-her-man kinda girl. I like getting my hands dirty. I prefer to have them in the mess helping to clean it up. But if you don't want my help, and you don't want to contribute any effort to this, I have to assume you already don't think I'm worth it and probably never will."

"I thought you might be upset, but I figured you'd at least be cool about it."

"Not-exclusive for *my* benefit isn't considerate; it's a cop-out that I'm not *cool* with. Relationships are filled with obstacles. I don't want to be with a guy who's gonna put me on the sideline and take off every time one arises."

"Now you're definitely not being cool!"

"So, what is being *cool* to you—sex with no strings? What do I get to be for the next few months—a fuck buddy?"

"Whatever—I have to go to work." Justin opens the front door.

"Don't you need a ride?"

"Tanzi just got here to pick me up—she's been texting." He slams the door.

Rachel stands in the middle of the living room mouth gaping. She waits a few moments hoping he'll come back and apologize or at least try to leave on better terms. Eventually, the gust of wind from the door turns stale and she stops hoping. She slumps down on the couch and sobs. Gasping for air, she wipes a river of snot on her favorite blanket, and wonders if going along with his *non-exclusive* plan would have been worth avoiding the horrible sense of finality that came after he slammed the door.

Her cell phone rings. Hoping it's him, she doesn't check the caller ID. She closes her eyes and answers with the calmest voice possible.

"What are you doing, freak!?" Sadie asks.

"Sorry I didn't call back last night, but I can't deal with you throwing a fit right now."

"I'm not *that* mad. I'm having a shit day, too. Scratch that, I'm having a shit year. No, wait—a shit life! Wanna wallow together?"

"As fun as that sounds, I have to work."

"Well, you have to at least hear about what happened to me last night!"

"Yeah?"

"Eric took me to a party, and then totally ditched me for some slutty bitch in a purple wig!"

"That's awful," Rachel says with as much revolt as she can muster. She gets ready for work half-listening to Sadie ramble about her horrible night, hearing enough to learn that purple-wig girl showed her boobs to everyone at the party, made out with some chick in the corner for an hour, then disappeared into the back room with two guys—one of whom was Eric.

"I'm really sorry, Sadie. He didn't seem like that kind of guy."

"I know—right!"

"I think maybe we should just swear off men completely for a while."

"I'm not ready to join a convent or go muff diving yet, but I would like to drown my sorrows and do some dancing." Sadie makes a snapping noise and Rachel knows she's shaking her hips.

Rachel envies Sadie's emotional elasticity when it comes to relationships. But she's also annoyed by Sadie's ability to be less emotionally invested. "Of course, you would!" Rachel says.

"What's that supposed to mean?"

Rachel sighs. "I'm just not up to going out tonight."

"Fine—whatever, I'll call one of my *fun* friends!"

Rachel knows Sadie is referring to one of the twits she was in interior design school with who still lives at home with her parents and has nothing better to spend money on than expensive underwear and alcohol. She used to cringe when Sadie made her compete with those girls. Now she welcomes the idea of someone else stepping in as Sadie's chauffeur for the penis-hunt and *me-me-me* stories. "Okay."

Sadie is stunned. It's the first time this manipulation hasn't worked; she sounds lost for an alternative. "I guess I'll just text you pics of how much fun we're having as we dance the night away."

"Have fun."

"Fine! You, too—Ms. Misery!"

Rachel hangs up and checks for missed calls. Nothing. Her chest hurts, and she wants to sit down on the couch and keep crying, but that would make her late for work—again, so she gulps down the pain and leaves. The ride to work is a blur of sporadic tears and motor-memory responses that ensure use of turn signals and windshield-wipers. She reruns the argument in her head and stews over whether she could or should have done anything different. The last guy who used the *let's-keep-it-casual* line, had cheated on her three times after finally agreeing to be exclusive. And both of the guys she had said that line to, were not guys she ever wanted to date exclusively. From her experience, that line is just another way to say *you're not good enough for me.*

Rachel ignores company policy by not having the radio on a local pop station. Sarah McLachlan's melancholy melodies fill the shop. She's drowning in rejection and escapes her misery by focusing on the pensive lyrics sung by the sultry voice while eating half a bowl of penis chocolates. She takes the small trash filled with incriminating pink and purple foil wrappers to the dumpster, but the extra effort to protect her job barely seems worth it. *Screw Justin and his misperceptions of her expectations.* She would have been happy to take it slow without giving him permission to be on the lookout for something better. But he had to go and shit all over it and now she feels more alone than before.

She always plays it safe and sticks with the *good* crowd. Now she wonders why. She wants a mind-numbing drug or alcohol addiction. She longs for any type of escape from the gnawing pain in her head and weight on her chest—no matter how irresponsible. Then everyone will have a legitimate reason to reject her. If she slams her head through the wall, she can blame it on the beer. If she jumps off the roof, she can blame it on drugs. Either way, at least she'll feel more alive. She's sick of worrying about wearing a condom to avoid contracting HIV or puss-filled genital sores. She wants to dig through a stranger's medicine cabinet or buy a handful of pills from the greasy-haired guy on the corner without having to worry about brain damage, teeth clenching, or tremors. She doesn't want to count calories anymore. And she's tired of worrying about finding a husband who will be faithful and a good father. She doesn't want to care about voting or laws. She wants to live in a world of chaos where just staying alive makes her a queen among scavengers. She imagines herself as a professional assassin with no conscience, prolific in martial arts and sexy in vinyl pants. She throws a punch and a kick, knocking over a rack of striped stockings, then remembers how sad she was when her dog died and thinks, who am I kidding?

As if being rejected by the best prospect she's had in years isn't bad enough, the number of couples browsing for sexual board games and perverted playing cards is unbearable. No matter how unconventional the purchase, people are always more comfortable in pairs; they're not shifty-eyed while paying; they hold their heads high when leaving; they don't pause to check the parking lot—making sure they won't run into someone they know while holding the conspicuous violet bag with the *I'm-a-freak-in-the-sack* logo. Like girls at a bar, confidence comes in pairs, and the porn shop is no exception. Usually couples bring a sense of respect to her job. Today they just seem snobbish and mocking of her failure to maintain a long-term relationship.

A young couple needing gag gifts for a friend's wedding ramble on about a jumping penis and a snow-globe with a prostitute on Santa's lap that someone had put in a gag gift for their wedding just a few months earlier. The girl—probably a year or two younger than Rachel—shows off her ring and sneaks a few lace G-strings into the purchase while her husband gawks at the Christmas tree shaped anal plug. They leave holding hands and Rachel crumples to the floor behind the cash register.

The bells on the door jingle. She wipes away tears and stands up thinking the obnoxiously happy couple forgot something. Instead, two thirty-something men stand at the front of the store joking about a pair of yellow latex chaps hanging on the wall.

"Welcome," she says in her standard, company-policy greeting voice with the biggest fake smile she can muster.

"Eeeeeek!" one of the men yells.

"Sorry, I was in the back."

"I would always be in the back if I worked in a store like this." He giggles and smacks the other man's ass.

"Mmmhhhmmm." His blue faux-hawked partner playfully reciprocates with a shoulder slug, then turns to Rachel. "I'm so sorry. I really can't take Ronnie anywhere."

"No worries, anything goes in here."

They both raise their eyebrows.

"Well, anything not requiring clothing removal."

"Naturally."

"Naaaturally," Ronnie repeats with a more exaggerated lisp than his partner while flinging a blue scarf over his shoulder.

Both men have soft features. They're wearing tight t-shirts that accentuate long muscle contour, but aren't wearing jackets, which seems peculiar on a cool, rainy day. Their oily brown skin smells like cocoa butter, so she assumes they just left the tanning salon across the street.

Ronnie points to the radio. "Why so Sarah?" He makes a pouty face. "Boy trouble?"

"Snoopy-face, leave the girl alone," Blue-faux-hawk says.

"He's right," Rachel says.

Ronnie beams. "Wanna talk about it?"

"Have mercy, Oprah is in the house!" Blue-faux-hawk throws his arms in the air and hides from Ronnie in the lingerie.

Rachel hesitates.

"Just spill it. I don't know much, but if there's anything I *do* know—it's boys." Ronnie makes a gimmie gesture with his hands.

"The guy I'm dating told me he wants to *keep it casual.*"

"Ouch." Ronnie says.

"That's not sooo bad," Blue-faux-hawk mutters from behind a silky purple bustier.

Ronnie scowls. "It is if you're in *luuuv!*"

"Are you in love?" Ronnie asks. "Scratch that—of course, you are! It's all over your puffy pink porcelain doll cheeks. I just want to strap you into a corset and have a tea party."

Rachel laughs.

"Someone else, or is he just a commitment-phobe?"

"Commitment-phobe," Rachel says.

"You need to say *hell no* to Mr. Keep-it-Casual."

"Done."

"Snap—you go, China-doll!" Ronnie makes a silent clapping gesture. "Now get in tight with his friends. And don't turn into a puddle of misery. Be fun. Be upbeat. Pop up enough that he can't get you out of his head, but not so much that he thinks about getting a restraining order."

"Been there!" Blue-faux-hawk yells from across the shop.

"And by all means, date someone else ASAP. If that's what he *really* wants, don't hesitate to show him what it feels like. I bet you just need to call his bluff—"

Rachel's phone rings.

Ronnie squeals. "Oh, my gawd I hope that's him! Is it him?"

"It's one of his friends."

"Okay, China-doll, that's a *must take*, so we're gonna skedaddle."

"I can't believe you just said skedaddle!" Blue-faux-hawk rushes for the door.

Ronnie attempts to wink but looks more like something is caught in his eye and gives her two-thumbs-up.

"Hola!" Rachel says.

"Cómo está usted!" Cerise replies.

"Sorry, you lost me at cómo."

Cerise laughs. "Busy tonight?"

Both of Rachel's raw eyelids and inflamed nostrils tell her to say she's busy, but Ronnie's advice is still buzzing in her head, and the glimmer of hope results in her saying, "Nope—what do you have in mind?"

"Yaaaaaaaay!" Cerise yells into the phone. "We're going to a paaaar-ty, and driiiiiin-ky, where everyone will beeee-ee." There's a muffled clang, a long beep, and Cerise yells, *"Shit!"* from far away. "Sorry, I dropped my phone. Whatever—you get the point."

"So, does everyone include Justin?" Rachel asks, then hiccups.

"I sent him a text, but he doesn't come to many of our big things. Maybe you can convince him to come?"

Rachel is relieved to hear that Cerise hasn't heard about their fight. "Sure, yeah—I'll call him."

The Light in the Sound

"Something wrong?"

"Nope."

"Okay, well, it's gonna be awesome, so wear something sparkly!"

Black Picket Fence

The address Cerise gave Rachel is on a dark street in a neighborhood she isn't familiar with, but the crooked rows of old cars on the dead lawn are a good indication she's at the right place. She parks near Cerise's red Volkswagen Bug—easily recognizable by the ladybug stickers in the back window. Two guys stumble out of the house; one guy's pants are already around his ankles and his underwear is catching up quick. She frowns at his bright-white ass. She hates this scene and plans to leave as soon as possible. They whistle at her, disappearing into the bushes to pee. She's surprised they still possess the continence to wait that long.

Abbie (one of Justin's friends from the night of Ian's show) is sitting on a faded-gold corduroy couch in the living room.

"Rachel—you came!" Abbie smiles and scoots to make her

a space to sit down.

Abbie's boyfriend, Kaleb, walks toward the couch holding two cans of beer. He spots Rachel next to Abbie, spins around on one heel, and heads back into the kitchen.

"Wow, I scared him off fast."

Abbie laughs. "Things still going good with Justin?"

"Eh, we had a rough morning."

"Justin is a tough case—hang in, but brace for impact."

Rachel nods and feels warm.

"If you *really* like him, don't give up. He's a good guy—too good in some ways."

"Sure, yeah." Rachel says.

Abbie looks down at her lap and sighs. "I probably shouldn't tell you this, but his ex-girlfriend cheated on him with his *brother*. I don't know if you've met Joel yet, but let me just say—*eww*."

Rachel isn't as shocked by the fact that Justin's ex-girlfriend cheated on him as she is that he went out with a girl willing to fuck someone as creepy and immature as Joel. She isn't sure if she should be sympathetic or concerned. Then she remembers the stupid slut her ex cheated on her with and decides to go with sympathy.

Kaleb reappears with three beers and hands a cold one to Rachel.

"Good man!" Abbie says.

Kaleb leans down and collects a kiss from Abbie in exchange for her beer, then crams his pointy hips in between them on the couch. Rachel is now squished against a balding stocky guy talking on his cell phone giving someone directions. He nods hello and his elbow grazes her breast.

She stands up to breathe.

"Punch my muscle!" a guy yells from across the room. Two guys are kneeling at the soot-burned hearth of a brown-brick fireplace. Both are flexing in an arm-wrestling stance, but not gripping hands. Instead, they're taking turns punching each other's muscles to watch them twitch. Rachel feels like she's in a bad eighties movie.

Abbie's golden curls bounce while she laughs at their antics. Kaleb pushes ringlets behind her ears, so she won't get beer in her hair.

Rachel wishes someone cared enough to protect her hair from sticky beer. "I'm gonna go find Cerise."

"Last I saw her, she was in the backyard." Abbie points to the sliding glass door.

Rachel holds her breath as she walks through a group of people smoking cigarettes on the patio. Half of which will likely die from a smoking-related illness and don't care. Not that she can read their minds, but their formaldehyde-scented hair and tar-stained teeth reek of adolescent omnipotence. A pasty-white girl with thick green eyeliner and coal-black hair purposely blows a cloud of smoke in Rachel's face. Her eyes burn, and she hopes that girl will be one of the five.

Small groups of people are scattered around the yard. A spray-tanned girl with short blonde hair bounces on one leg while stripping, then jumps in the gray marble hot tub housed in a cherry-wood gazebo. Two guys knee deep in water—wearing nothing but boxer shorts, are holding up beer cans and cheering. Another girl about to jump in, trips on a sprinkler and stumbles forward. Her white cotton bikini panties ride up her orange ass revealing a small red heart tattoo centered on her left cheek. The cheering grows louder and Rachel shrugs off an invitation to join them as she walks by.

Tiki torches line the path to a dripping wet patio table covered in beer cans, hard liquor bottles, and a chrome keg. Cerise is standing near the table beneath an archway wrapped in strands of white twinkle lights; dots of light form constellations on her cheeks. Cerise squeals when she sees Rachel, throwing her arms out for a hug. Pink drink sloshes out of a clear cup, landing on her black velvet ballerina shoes, but she doesn't notice, or is too drunk to care. Either way, Rachel is flattered by her excitement.

"Did you see the hottie in the hot tub?" Cerise asks as she points.

The guy in the hot tub jumps up, bends over, and shakes his ass for attention.

Cerise puts two fingers in her mouth and whistles.

"He seems a little preoccupied with the Oompa Loompa," Rachel says.

"She'll be passed out by ten. Sandy—I mean, Oompa Loompa—can't hold her liquor. Doesn't matter, he's my plan-B anyway."

"Oh yeah, who's plan-A?"

Cerise does a slow, low laugh and finishes the remainder of her drink. She reaches into her pocket and pulls out a clear baggy. Inside are a matching pair of small round pink pills etched with a butterfly design. She hands them to Rachel. "Plan-A," she says.

"What's this?"

"Shut the fuck up! Do *not* tell me you work in a porn shop

and have never done *X*!"

"Okay, I won't tell you."

"I don't usually push drugs, but you're seriously missing out. You've *got* to try it *at least* once."

Rachel stares at the pale-pink pills rolling around inside the baggy, seemingly as harmless as Flintstones vitamins. She thinks back on the public service commercials she had watched as a kid during after-school specials where a long-haired guy in a torn t-shirt with dirty fingernails hung around the fence at a schoolyard trying to sell drugs. The *cool* kids always said *no* in a confidently defiant way that adults assumed would make other children want to imitate; the same way they had all been influenced to beg their parents for pressurized-air water guns, and miniature microwave ovens to nuke brownies that tasted like cocoa chewing gum. But the anti-drug ads just made her laugh. Even while growing up in a devoutly religious community, illegal drugs were readily available—and it wasn't because greasy guys were lurking in the shadows. Most of it trickled down from the older siblings or parents of the "cool" kids. She avoided drugs by simply acting disinterested. And despite never having done anything but smoke marijuana a few times, she'd been accused of being addicted to everything.

When her grades started slipping because her parents moved twice during one school year, it had to be drugs. When her mom was too depressed to do laundry for weeks and she wore her nightshirt, torn up jeans, and bunny slippers to school, it had to be drugs. When she stopped going to church, there was no way that her father was knocking her around at night after purporting as the guiding light of God by day.

Nope, it had to be drugs. When she left home at sixteen because she'd come home early from work one afternoon and overheard her stepmother on the phone lying in an attempt to have her locked in a juvenile detention facility; it couldn't have been because Rachel mustered the strength to finally call the police after her dad threw her down the stairs the night before, it had to be drugs. And of course, when she got her first tattoo—two years later—it had to be drugs.

For over ten years, she'd been accused of being addicted to everything imaginable. All the while, every adult in her life popped their legal form of escapism, neatly packaged in a small prescription bottle handed over with a smile by a clean-cut person in a long white jacket who went to college and never lingered around schoolyard fences in faded, glam-rock t-shirts. Never once had she done anything as addictive, mood altering, or dangerous as the pills that rolled around in those little brown bottles, but somehow, *she* was the delinquent addict. Her parents were so wrong about her, it made all the other accusations easier to ignore. She had avoided drugs because validating their presumptions might somehow justify the lies and abuse. Being so rejected and consequently alone was difficult, but the inaccurate reasons why had never been her burden to bear. But she's so disconnected from that world now it really doesn't matter. There is nothing left to prove. She's alone and has been for so long, there is only the nagging sense of endless rejection to keep her company.

Deep down she knows she'll find her tattooed prince charming and have a black picket fence one day, but every failed attempt numbs her to the prospect. Hope no longer feels like a renewable commodity the way it did as a child.

Each year it's drowned out by more harsh reality. If nothing else, she just wants to feel alive again. Even if the high sucks, swallowing the pink pill will be a new experience, and the excitement in that prospect alone sounds more enticing than saying *no thank you* and going home to hangout with Ewoka all night, alone. She shrugs, hands the baggie back, and says, "Sure, I'm in."

"Weeeeeeeee." Cerise twirls in a circle. "We should stop drinking now. I dated a biology major who told me alcohol mixed with *X* fucks with your homeostasis and causes stuff like dehydration. All I know for sure—from trying it both ways—is that it's way better without it cuz alcohol dilutes the high and makes the come-down worse. Just stop drinking now and you'll be good. I'll stop, too. This is only like my second drink anyway."

Rachel puts her beer down and plays along.

"I don't think we should do it here, though. My first time was pretty intense and the last thing we want is to sit through one of Abbie's anti-drug lectures while we're high. I say we hangout here for a couple more hours, then go to your place. Cool? Oh, and I actually came here with five pills, but I sold three already: one to the hottie in the hot tub; one to one of his buddies; and one to an old friend of mine who I'm trying to set up with his buddy. Is it ok if I tell them we can all crash at your place?"

"Sure, yeah."

"That's cool, really?"

"Totally."

Normally, Rachel would have been annoyed by people she doesn't know coming over, but she's sick of being a loner and just wants to roll with it.

"I knew this was going to be a good night!"

"You do have *happy* in a baggie."

"Yeah, but you don't want to do good drugs with bad people. Trust me—it's all about the company."

The next two hours are a blur of fake laughs and awkward introductions. Rachel meets nearly everyone Justin has ever known and asks Cerise (twice) to stop introducing her as his girlfriend. "We're not doing the titles thing," she said. "I don't know if we're even still dating—probably not," she finally admits, fearful that saying she isn't good enough for Justin might make her seem not good enough for his friends.

"Are you serious!?" Cerise yells, causing people to stare.

"I really don't want to talk about it," Rachel says.

"Fuck it—let's get out of here." Cerise wades through swarms of people to find her pill buddies while Rachel waits by her car near a guy passed out in the bushes. She's happy to escape the cigarette clouds, body odor, and witless anecdotes. She counts twelve crooked parking jobs, two empty cigarette boxes, and fourteen scattered butts. Moaning comes from the backseat of a blue hatchback parked in front of her. She looks up at the stars and wonders what Justin is doing. The couple in the hatchback get progressively louder, giggling, squealing, and rolling around, pounding on the side window yelling, "Go baby—go!" Rachel pulls her knee-length sweater jacket tighter around her waist and checks her phone for missed calls. Nothing.

Cerise finally exits the house with three drunk people in tow, and Rachel hears her lecturing about a shitty high.

"These are my dumbass friends, Peter, Evan, and Tina," she says, but all Rachel remembers is, Plaid, Pac-Man, and Pink-stripe. Plaid (who spent all night at the hot tub in his red and green plaid boxer shorts yelling at girls to join him) smells like chlorine. His neck is tinted orange and she assumes its spray-tan residue, but his whole complexion is a little blotchy. Now that she's seen him up close, she's even more confused about Cerise thinking he's attractive. But blonds—and guys who try to round up girls like cattle—have never been Rachel's type, so she chalks it up to the expensive clothes and shoes. Evan is wearing a faded-blue, Pac-Man t-shirt—big shocker. He's tan with a dark, clear complexion, blue eyes, and thick, dark brown hair in a bed-head-do with nice sheen. He also has a kind smile and when he reaches out to shake her hand he flexes, accentuating bicep contour that shows he cares but isn't a gym-junky. Tina has a pointy nose and is so skinny Rachel is afraid to shake her hand for fear of breaking it. But she likes the pink-stripe in her platinum-blonde hair and bracelet tattoo of black swirls climbing up her forearm to her elbow, so she decides not to judge the pointy red heels, skinny jeans, and tight checkered button-up shirt that's a little too cowgirl-hooker for Rachel's taste. "Who's riding with me and who's riding with Cerise?"

"Is this *your* car?" Plaid asks.

"Why?"

"Because I think I love you," he says, runs up to the front of the Charger and dry-humps the hood. "I'm riding with you and you're giving me the keys."

"Sorry, buddy—that's definitely *not* happening." Rachel shakes her head and rolls her eyes.

Plaid makes a pouty face.

"You're so fucking wasted," Pac-Man says. "I wouldn't even let you ride my bike—just get in the car and shut up."

Plaid sticks his middle finger up his nose, drops his shoulders, and drags his feet to the passenger side.

"I guess I'll ride with Rachel to keep him in check," Pac-Man says.

"Then I'm with Cerise," Pink-stripe says, locking arms with her as they walk away.

"I have no idea where we're going, so don't lose me," Cerise yells over her shoulder.

"Lose her—I dare you," Plaid says after Cerise is out of earshot.

"I thought you were friends," Rachel says.

"Yeah, we're cool. But Cerise's appetite is voracious and I'm not one to go back for sloppy seconds—if you know what I mean." He nudges Rachel with his elbow and has a wide-eyed expression that makes him look like an albino praying mantis.

"I see," Rachel says, but she isn't referring to his stupid comment—what she really sees is a jackass, and she can't comprehend why the hell Cerise wants to hook up with him. She thinks about getting on the freeway and pushing Plaid out of the car, but he's so dumb she could probably just roll down the window and he'd fall out on his own.

Pac-Man smacks him on the back of the head. "It's not like that. He's full of shit. Just ignore him."

"Whatever, dude—you're just pissed cuz I got Cerise first."

"As if, man—I wouldn't touch anything your dick was near."

"Then you better stop kissing your mom goodnight." Plaid smacks his own leg as he spit-laughs all over the dash.

Rachel hopes she won't get high enough to consider doing anything with this loser.

"We could always just leave you here," Pac-Man says, making eye contact with Rachel through the rearview mirror and winking.

She laughs. For the first time all night, she doesn't care about checking her phone for missed calls.

Plaid rolls down the window and hangs his head out. "Are we there yet—I need to pee."

Rachel peels out.

Everyone piles into Rachel's apartment and lingers in the living room. The room seems smaller than usual and she realizes that this is the most people she's ever had over at one time. She instructs everyone to hang their jackets on a coat hanger she had painted to look like a tree. Rachel gives a mini-tour—mostly to point out the bathroom—and tells everyone to make themselves comfortable.

Cerise opens the fridge and starts passing around cans of cola. "Let's get this party started." She opens the baggy and pulls out a pill, handing it to Rachel. "These damn things can take a while to kick in. I've heard Molly is a better high, but we're not that *connected*." Everyone laughs. "No worries, though, this is the same stuff I took last time and it kicks ass."

"Yeah, it better not be as bad as the blue-diamonds we took Labor Day weekend," Plaid says, then swallows his pill.

"Better high?" Rachel asks.

"Most pills are cut with caffeine, ephedrine, speed, or

other psychoactive amphetamines," Cerise says.

Rachel has no idea what that means and doesn't want to know. If she did, she'd probably never partake. She's the last one to take her pill and stalls as long as possible to make sure no one starts foaming at the mouth. She considers fake swallowing but decides it's too late to turn back now. There's no candy coating, and the chalky pill goes down slow and hard. Probably the same way it's going to hit her brain, she thinks.

"Thanks for letting us all crash here," Pac-Man says.

Rachel points to the hall closet. "Blankets are in there and I think I have a sleeping bag—we'll figure it out."

"Yeah, we'll figure it out." Pac-Man smiles and holds eye contact.

"Whatever!" Cerise yells. Guys are out here—girls are in the bedroom."

"Come on!" Plaid says. "That bed is big enough for *at least* five people."

"Keep dreamin'," Rachel says, jumping because her phone rings. Her heart races and she wonders if she's high, but it slows to normal pace and she realizes she's still very sober. Assuming it's Sadie, she finally looks at the caller ID, freezing when she sees Justin's number. "I'll be right back." She walks outside. The cool night air smacks her warm cheeks.

"Hey," Justin says.

"Hey."

Long pause.

"Soooooo I'm sorry about earlier. I think it all just came out *really* wrong," he says slowly.

"Yeah, me too."

"I don't want to stop seeing you. But if you don't want to see me anymore, I really don't want it to end like that."

Rachel agrees, and notices Cerise peeking out the window. Despite walking outside in just her t-shirt, she's warming up, or the air has warmed up. All she knows for sure is that the champagne-orange patio light makes everything look warm and cozy and she wants to curl up under the nearest tree and count stars. She looks up, but thin gray clouds obstruct the view, so she tallies cracks in the sidewalk.

"You there?"

"Sorry, I'm tired," Rachel says.

"Can I come over, so we can talk?"

She glances at the clock on her phone and wonders where he's been all night. Plus, she's on the brink of turning into a bowl of Jell-O. "I think we need to just get some sleep and talk again tomorrow."

"But we'll talk tomorrow, right?" The desperation in his voice is tainted with guilt that Rachel thinks has to do with more than just this morning.

"Have a good night."

"You too."

She lingers outside and looks around, but nothing seems quite as psychedelic as it did a few minutes ago.

Cerise is cross-legged on the couch next to Pink-stripe who is drawing tree branches up her own arm with a red pen. Plaid and Pac-Man are sitting on the floor playing a video game on an old console that one of Sadie's *flings* had brought over and never came back to claim. "Anyone feeling anything yet?" Rachel asks.

"Nope," everyone responds one after the other.

"You?" Pac-Man asks Rachel.

"I thought maybe, but I guess not."

Cerise laughs. "Oh, you'll know."

"Shouldn't be long now," Plaid says. His character—a tall blonde in a tight pink dress—throws a burst of blue energy at Pac-Man's character—a small orange dinosaur that subsequently dies. Pac-Man punches Plaid in the arm.

Rachel puts her hand out, signaling Pac-Man to pass the controller so she can obliterate Plaid on the only video game she's good at playing. But her heart races and stomach gets queasy, then everything starts spinning. "I don't feel so good," she says, sitting down on the floor.

"Uh-oh, newbie alert," Plaid says.

"Shut up!" Cerise smacks Plaid where Pac-Man just punched him, and he winces. "I forgot to ask if you'd eaten'," she says.

"Not since breakfast," Rachel says.

Pac-Man jumps up, runs into the kitchen, and comes back with a glass of water. "Here, just take slow deep breaths and drink this."

She's short of breath and every movement is labored. Her head and chest are in a war over which one gets to explode first, and her body can't decide whether it's warm or cold.

"She's pretty green," Pink-stripe says from a couple of feet away.

Though she might as well be in the next room because Rachel can only see the blurry people right in front of her. Peripheral movement is too much to process. She closes her eyes to block it out.

"Can you make her a sandwich?" she hears Cerise ask.

"Sure," Pac-Man says.

She prays they know what they're doing because she refuses to let this be the way she goes out and is on the brink of dialing 9-1-1.

Pac-Man returns with a quartered turkey sandwich and sits cross-legged in front of her. He hands her a square. "Eat this and look at me."

It's difficult to focus on something so close, so she stares at an enlarged photograph of Seattle hanging on the wall behind him. She'd taken the photo one night from Alki Beach, trying to capture the bold stripes of the city lights—yellow, red, green, teal, orange—reflecting in the Sound. The pressure in her head, rising and falling like a percussion instrument responding on cue to her irregular heart-rate, makes it difficult to make out anything other than the sea of stripes. Slowly counting the bright stripes of light in the Sound helps to bring the crisp lines of the structures they represent into focus, and she becomes slightly less fearful that her life is about to end. He urges her to eat the sandwich. She takes a small bite. Chewing is strained. She can't really taste the sandwich, but she knows it's soft and she's swallowing. If she were the normal kind of sick, she'd never eat right now. But everyone circles round, and every bite makes them all seem relieved, as if her dedication to the sandwich indicates there won't be any emergency-room visits to ruin the night. She hiccups and another wave of hot then cold rushes over her.

"Just look at me," Pac-Man repeats. She watches the large yellow pie chart that's about to swallow the small gray ghost on his shirt. He gently guides her chin upward. She follows the end of his crooked nose up to his forehead. Ribbons of yellow in his irises look like ridges on blue and white speckled seashells. Every time he blinks, his pupils get larger until only a small ring of blue frames a large black pupil and his eyes look like a pair of miniature solar eclipses. She's mesmerized by the metamorphosis. She can feel his warm, peppermint-schnapps scented breath on her nose. His cheeks flush bright red, then all color disappears; his face is left gaunt and drawn. Then, as quickly as it erupted, all sickness subsides, and she feels calmer than she's ever felt—like lying on the beach in warm sand on a breezy, sunny day—but better. Pac-Man smiles.

She looks around at her fellow smiling zombies with eclipsed eyes and thinks that they all seem like a new race of humanoid. They're all so eager to ensure she's okay, like paler, happy versions of their generally angst-ridden selves. Her head isn't cluttered with a million thoughts; each one occupies its own large space. And she's never been so aware of and in love with every aspect of existence. She thinks this is the closest she'll ever come to emotional utopia.

"Really, everybody, I'm okay," Rachel says. "Shit, I'm better than okay." She hugs Pac-Man, thanks him for the sandwich, stands up, hugs Cerise, and thanks her for the pill.

Plaid and Pac-Man smile at each other. Pac-Man grabs Plaid's hand to shake, pulling him in for a hug. "It's gonna be a good night," Pac-Man says.

"Hell yeah," Plaid says.

"I'm sorry I punched you, man," Pac-Man says.

"It's totally cool. I was being a jerk."

"I love all the colors in your apartment—great energy,"

Pink-stripe says to Rachel.

"Makes me want to paint," Cerise says.

"Your body?" Plaid asks.

Pink-stripe giggles.

Ewoka wanders in from the bedroom, looks around at everyone, then stretches and yawns so wide they can see the dark freckles on her long pink tongue.

"What color is my cat's aura?" Rachel asks Cerise.

Cerise squints at Ewoka. "Green," she finally says.

"Is that because her eyes are green?" Pac-Man asks.

"Huh?" Cerise looks confused.

"Sorry, I'm not questioning your ability. I just don't know how aura reading works, so I thought it might correspond with eye color or something?"

"Shit." Cerise shrugs. "Honestly, I have no idea what color the cat's aura is."

"A cat probably isn't like reading a person," Rachel says.

"Actually, it probably is. I just can't really see auras," Cerise says. "When I was a kid I called everyone colors in-stead of their names, so my mom got the big idea that I could see auras and it made me feel so special I played along. Now it's turned into this huge thing that somehow defines *her* identity, so I can't tell her it's not true. I studied aura reading, though. It's pretty easy to make up colors for people after you have a conversation with them. I can generally tell what they want to hear."

Pac-Man raises his hand to speak. Everyone stares and waits. "I'm gay," he finally says.

"I knew it," Plaid yells.

"No, you didn't," Pac-Man says.

"You're right—I didn't." Plaid hangs his head, and Pac-Man pats him on the back.

"Well, my high just peeked," Pink-stripe says.

"Sorry," Pac-Man says.

"Sorry," Pink stripe says to Plaid.

"It's no secret I'm a man-whore," Plaid says.

"That explains why a mechanic has such manicured hands," Pink-stripe says.

"You're a mechanic?" Cerise asks.

"Yeah, I was gonna tell Rachel earlier that if she wants to come in, I can fix the squeaky belt on her car—no charge."

Rachel smiles.

"I'm a plumbing apprentice. Do you have any leaky faucets?" Plaid asks Rachel.

"Not that I know of."

"I think we should all go stand in the bathtub and find out," Plaid says.

"Huh?" the girls say in unison.

"Don't go perving out on me now, ladies, just keep your clothes on—it'll be fun. Unless of course you *want* to take your clothes off, then don't let me stop you." Plaid smiles and beckons toward the bathroom.

Euphoric curiosity compels them to follow.

Plaid runs just enough warm water to cover their feet and ankles. Everyone rolls up their pant legs and steps in. It's a tight fit, but they pull it off with Pac-Man sitting on the side. Plaid grabs a bottle of sweet-orange and vanilla organic shampoo, pops it open and takes a whiff. "Yum," he says, passing the bottle around. Everyone agrees. Pac-Man peels off the back portion of the yellow label with the company name and puts it in his pocket.

"You can have the bottle," Rachel says.

"This is all I need." He smiles.

"Check it out," Pink-stripe says as she points to the water. "Our different colored toenails look like little fish."

Cerise wiggles her pink fish while Pink-stripe wiggles her teal-blue fish and Rachel wiggles her purple fish. They have fish wars until Plaid laughs so hard he almost pees and has to get out. Pac-Man pulls the seashell shower curtain shut, giving Plaid some privacy, but as soon as he starts peeing, Cerise announces that she's found a leaky faucet. Pac-Man laughs so hard he falls backward, pulling the shower curtain and plastic rod down on Plaid.

"Ahhhhhh," Plaid says, stumbling around trying to untangle himself from the shower curtain, then runs into the wall.

Pink-stripe hops out to help Plaid while Rachel and Cerise almost fall out of the tub as well.

Rachel passes around a towel for everyone to dry their feet. She experiences a wave of nausea, followed by a momentary mood plunge. It's a scary, overwhelming urge to cry, and she fears it portends what's to come when the high subsides, but she feels happy again so quickly, she doesn't mention it.

Pac-Man turns the oven up to 400 degrees and pops open the door to warm his hands.

"Sorry, I can turn the heat up," Rachel says.

"Nah—this is great," he says. Putting his arm around her shoulder, he pulls her close.

Rachel enjoys affection from someone not expecting sex. It's like being hugged by a brother or an old friend for just being her. And not because it's the well-timed, polite thing to do, but because they want their energy to connect with hers to communicate with something stronger than words that she's a member of their inner circle and welcome in their personal space. It's a genuine moment that doesn't last long enough because Cerise squeezes between them and rests her head on Rachel's shoulder.

Everyone gathers around the oven and puts their hands out as if huddled over a campfire. The pale-yellow walls glow in the soft light. Eventually, they all pull up chairs and talk for hours about everything from their favorite kind of pie to why Pink-stripe gained weight in high school, which is hard to believe because she's so thin now. She's convinced it was to avoid having sex with boys because her uncle was slipping into her room at night when he visited her family every summer. Plaid threatens to kill him, but she says he fell off a ladder and died last summer. Everyone agrees that karma paid him a visit. Plaid offers to dig him up and kill him again anyway. Pink-stripe laughs and says his death had brought her peace because he had a young daughter and now she knows he'll never be able to do the same thing to her. They all hug her and sit in silence.

"I think I get tattoos to hide now," Pink-stripe says.

"Really?" Plaid says. "I always thought people got tattoos to standout or something."

"After I started getting tattooed, people couldn't see me anymore—all they see are the tattoos and the person they *assume* that makes me, so I hide under my ink."

Rachel pulls up her pant leg to show the Asian dragon on her left ankle. Cerise and Pac-Man take turns rubbing the smooth blue skin.

Pac-Man stands up and pulls off his shirt revealing a large, detailed oak tree covering most of his back. In between the branches are random words and phrases. "It's mostly song lyrics or reminders of inspiring moments," he says. He flexes his shoulders and the boughs bulge with life.

Rachel has never wanted to lick someone's skin more, but she somehow refrains—even though she's pretty sure he won't mind. At least if he feels as good as she does. Instead, she softly glides her fingers down his back. "It's so beautiful," she says, mesmerized by the story on his skin.

"I saw the trees you painted in your bedroom, they're really good." He turns around and opens his mouth to say more but stops himself. Rachel holds her breath hoping he'll continue, but he never does. She remembers the downer wave she had in the bathroom and assumes he's experiencing the same, so she just says, "Thank you." And sits back down.

"I miss Ian," Cerise says.

"That guy is a douche-bag," Plaid says, "You can do better."

"I agree," Pink-stripe says.

"Do you think it's possible to die of a broken heart?" Cerise asks.

"Definitely," Pink-stripe says. "I read an article that said stress weakens your heart making you more prone to a heart attack, but I think it's more applicable when someone you love dies or something extreme like that. I don't think it would apply to just breaking up with a loser."

"I don't know," Plaid says. "It was pretty intense when my girlfriend dumped me. My sis had me on suicide-watch for days."

Pink-stripe gives him a hug, then kisses his pale, freckled nose. Everyone's spellbound waiting for their next move. Finally, they kiss. Paralyzed, like never having seen two people kiss before, they all linger in the moment, living vicariously through Pink-stripe and Plaid's outstretched lips and dancing noses. Until they bow their heads in reverence, as if part of a collective unconscious.

Cerise stands up and announces she's going to bed.

Pink-stripe and Plaid separate. "Sorry," Pink-stripe says softly.

"No apologies," Cerise says. She opens the closet and pulls out a stack of blankets.

"I'm gonna crash out here," Pink-stripe says.

"I know," Cerise says. Walking into the living room, she starts laying out a blanket bed.

"You're on your own," Cerise says to Pac-Man, handing him the sleeping bag.

Pac-Man walks up to Rachel. "I'm really glad we met."

"Me too." Rachel smiles and stares up into his eyes—still eclipsed but showing more blue than earlier. She wishes he wasn't gay.

He leans down and kisses the side of her face, lingering. His soft warm cheek is pressed against hers and she can feel his breath in her ear. He seems nervous and she swears he says something, but she can't make it out, so she pulls back and whispers, "What?"

"Sleep well," he says coolly and walks away.

That wasn't it! It didn't sound anything like that. Her hope sinks, thinking she missed something important. "You too," she says, apologetically.

Cerise grabs Rachel's arm and drags her into the bedroom. "Come on—sleepy bye, beddy bye."

Rachel looks down and realizes Plaid and Pink-stripe are on the verge of tearing each other's clothes off. "Are you sure we shouldn't let him crash in here with us?" Rachel asks.

"He's a big boy, he'll be juuuuust fine," Cerise says, closing the door behind her. She wastes no time stripping off her clothes and climbing under the blanket. "I can't sleep in clothes, hope you don't mind."

Normally, Rachel is self-conscious about taking her clothes off in front of anyone, but she feels so confident and sure of herself right now that she could probably grocery shop naked. She loves the feel of soft fabrics, so she slips into a pair of pale blue silk shorts and a white cotton tank top, then climbs into bed facing Cerise. There are three-inches of foam on the mattress beneath her purple sheets and she sinks into it thinking she's never loved her bed so much.

"I used your toothbrush," Cerise says.

"What a coincidence, I used my toothbrush, too!"

The curtains are open and early morning light peeks through cracks in the window blinds giving everything a pale-blue hue.

"You look like Smurfette," Cerise says.

"Thanks...I think."

"Smurfette is cute."

Rachel smiles.

Cerise runs her finger across Rachel's mouth. "I love your thick, pouty bottom lip."

Rachel isn't sure if she wants this, but she knows she doesn't *not* want it. She loves the attention and she's attracted to Cerise, so she must be into girls more than she had previously considered. Cerise's fingers are small and her skin is soft. Her touch is gentle. Rachel knows that normally she'd be far too afraid of rejection and apprehensive about making a fool of herself, so she decides to seize the drug-induced, insouciant moment. She hops-up on her knees, conquers the wobble in the squishy bed, then climbs on top of Cerise, pinning her pale-blue arms to the purple pillow above her head. "You want this?"

Cerise nods.

Rachel leans down and presses her mouth to Cerise's strawberry-flavored lips, slowly opening her mouth just enough for their tongues to touch. They kiss softly for a few minutes, until Rachel realizes that she's holding back the same way she had during her first kiss in junior high with the high school boy she had ditched school to hangout with one day. Years later, she's been with enough boys, guys, then men, to have perfected her tongue swirls, lip sucking and taunting bites that left one guy's bottom lip bright blue and swollen. So why is she holding back with Cerise? She doesn't believe any of the religious bigotry preaching that she'll go to hell. All of a sudden, it hits her: Cerise isn't just a drugged-up, experimental make-out session with some random person. Rachel *really* likes Cerise; the same way she likes all of the men she's been with—if not more.

Cerise presses up and Rachel's entire body responds. It's the most united her mind and body have ever been during sex. Every inch is accounted for and completely present. She knows it's because of the little pink pill, but she doesn't care. She traces figure eights with her tongue on Cerise's neck, lifting her shirt and moving down her chest where she pauses, mesmerized by the near perfect replica of what men see when exploring her own body. Imitating the better of the bunch, she cups a handful of Cerise's breast, circling and flicking hard nipple with her tongue, slowly creating a two-inch wide trail of saliva down her stomach. Cerise wraps her thighs around Rachel's head and doesn't release until her back arches and the sheets bunch inside her clenched fists. They grind like teenagers dry-humping in the backseat of a car, kissing and exploring each other's bodies until Rachel's tongue is raw and her jaw aches. Eventually, she has to pee so bad that she can't delay anymore and promises to hurry back.

Rachel smoothes her hair and throws her shirt and shorts back on—just in case Plaid and Pink-stripe are still awake doing the same thing. She slips out of the bedroom and tiptoes across the kitchen into the bathroom. All is quiet until she flushes the toilet and opens the door. Pac-Man is standing in the hallway yawning, wearing nothing but his gray boxer briefs.

"Morning, sunshine," he says with a crooked, sleepy-eyed smile.

Rachel is self-conscious about the conspicuous layer of sweat coating her arms and legs, and she knows how swollen her bright-red lips are because she just finished gawking at herself in the mirror, but he doesn't seem to notice—or just doesn't care. He slips in while she's still standing in the doorway, lingering for a long, uncomfortable moment. She moves to clear the path.

"Hey," she says.

He struggles to hold his eyes open. "Yeah."

"Never mind." She shakes her head dismissively.

He grabs her arm. "No—what?" He's suddenly very awake and his grasp is firm.

"I'm just wondering what you said earlier...In my ear—I swear you said something."

He moves in close. She holds her breath. "I said," he pauses..."I lied." He grabs the back of her head and presses his mouth hard against hers. She would reciprocate, but her lips are almost numb. He lets go and jumps back, as if expecting to be slapped.

She opens her mouth to respond but nothing comes out. For the first time all night, she's speechless. She doesn't know whether she feels angry, betrayed, turned-on, or completely made a fool of, so she turns around and walks straight back to the bedroom. She finds Cerise still naked and passed out— about to roll off the side of the bed. After scooting her into the middle, Rachel sits on the side of the bed and stares at an empty space on the wall until she can't hold her eyes open anymore, then curls up in a ball with her pillow next to Cerise and falls asleep.

Jailbird

Rachel feels something soft on her face and opens her eyes to find she's touching noses with Cerise who looks like a green-eyed Owl Monkey. Rachel jumps back.

Cerise giggles, rubs her eyes, and sits up. "Morning."

Rachel is too disoriented to laugh. Her head feels heavy and waking up to Cerise lying naked beside her prompts a pause to assess how she feels—as if expecting to be flooded with the sensation of having done something horribly wrong, but it never comes.

Cerise holds up a business card pinched between two fingers. "What's this?"

"A business card."

She smirks and hands it over. "Funny."

Pac-Man's name and contact info for the auto repair shop where he works is on the front. Rachel flips it over and sees

Sorry scribbled on the back.

"I found it on the bathroom mirror. What's that all about?"

Rachel shrugs. She's annoyed by Cerise's jealousy and doesn't know how to respond. Rachel would hang back as long as possible, watching how it played out before demanding explanations. But Cerise's instincts are so accurate, Rachel feels compelled to confess, until she remembers the baseball bat in Ian's windshield.

"Sorry," Cerise says.

"It's cool. I get it."

"Do you?" Cerise stares searchingly.

Rachel's corneas are letting in way too much light and the bright, midday sun makes her head throb. She squints. "I get it."

Cerise smiles. "You should totally take a drag off one of my cigarettes. It'll give you a wicked buzz."

"Nah, I'm good."

"You like coffee?"

"Sure, yeah."

"It'll do the same. I want a blueberry muffin, too. We'll go to my favorite place. You're driving, though. I gave my keys to Tina."

"Cool." Rachel glances at her phone: one missed call from Justin, nine missed calls from Sadie, two new voice-mails—she ignores it all.

The dim light in the dark café is a welcomed break from the vibrant sun. Sluggish people create the order line while groups of two and three buzzing with conversation sit at small round tables. The scent of mocha is invigorating. Thank

God for legal drugs, she thinks. Cerise stands uncomfortably close and tries to hold Rachel's hand a couple of times, both of which Rachel casually pulls away from with a subtle gesture, like scratching her nose. She looks around to see if anyone is watching, but no one seems to notice that they even exist. They sit down with their drinks and muffins at a table in the corner with a purple and green dragonfly mosaic top. Halfway through the Caramel Macchiato, Rachel gets a buzz that doesn't come close to the previous night but puts alcohol to shame. She has an urge to rub the fuzzy green artificial leaves wrapped around a cast-iron lamppost standing in the corner near their table, and she struggles to sit still.

"So...I had a lot of fun last night," Cerise says.

Rachel creates a mustache with the velvety white cream on her drink and smiles.

Cerise smirks. "Be serious—I really want to talk about this."

"I'm here." Rachel wipes her mouth.

Cerise stares down at her drink. "I really like you—like a lot."

"Good, cuz I think I like you more than a lot."

Cerise smiles. "I feel like I can trust you, Rachel. I feel like I can be honest with you and you won't judge me."

Rachel hears the disclaimer surfacing and braces for impact.

Cerise holds her hand out straight. Rachel watches the tremors for a few seconds before Cerise pulls her sweatshirt sleeves over her fists, retracting like a turtle into its shell.

"Shit," Rachel says.

"Yeah, I'm pretty messed up. But you—and the hope of

an *us*, inspires me to get my shit together. I know I need to fix it on my own—I need to quit for good. But I'm gonna be pretty scary for a while. I just need to know you won't shut me out."

Cerise's desperation is intense. Rachel smiles and reaches across the table to squeeze her hand. "Bring me your worst. I can handle it."

Cerise takes a deep breath. "I can do this," she says—as if trying to convince herself now.

Rachel's phone rings.

"Where the freaking, fucking, flying hell have you been!?" Sadie screams from the other end of the call, then whispers, "Sorry" to someone else.

"Great to hear from you, too," Rachel says.

"You need to come pick me up."

"Where's your car?"

"Impounded!" she yells. "Yeah, yeah, yeah, I heard you the first time," she says to the other person.

"Where are you?" Rachel asks.

"I'm in the downtown Tacoma jail."

"Shut the fuck up!" Now people *are* staring. Rachel walks outside. Cerise follows. "It will take me like forty minutes to get down there, but I'm coming."

"You better be!" Sadie hangs up.

Five stories of portentous concrete shadows the parking lot. Rows of small, rectangle, leaded-glass windows barely humanize the structure that otherwise would be a monolith of misery. Rachel wonders how many people are sitting in cells for using or selling the drug that's still in her brain making her want to hug the security guard searching her purse. Cerise is especially uncomfortable with the scrutiny and decides to wait outside. Rachel watches her through the tinted-glass doors pacing under the octagon wing overhang as she lights up a cigarette and fidgets with her canvas bag. Cerise is the same mess she's been since the first night they met, but back then she was an anonymous mess—the kind Rachel could be intrigued and amused by from a safe distance without consequence or responsibility. Now that she's Rachel's mess, it doesn't seem so sexy.

The small elevator smells like new tires and industrial glue. She exits onto the third floor and nods to two square-chested female officers with tight ponytails who avoid eye contact and reciprocate with a quick flick of the chin, obviously disinterested in anyone not wearing handcuffs. Rachel rounds a corner and sees Sadie walking toward her.

"Finally!" Sadie yells. "Where the hell were you all night?" The smeared mascara under her eyes makes her look like a raccoon on meth. Her clothes have the stretched out, worn for way too long look, and she's missing one earring.

"My phone was dead."

"Yeah—I'm sure. So all I've had to do is think about how much my best friend sucks, which you really do you know— you suck!"

"It's not like you don't have other friends you could have called."

"Their mom's all hangout with my mom and the last thing I need is my dad finding out about this. He's ready to disown me already."

"Plus, you look like shit."

"Ya think!" She tries to smooth her hair, which is futile without a shower, an entire can of mousse, and a flat-iron. "What's with the shades?" She pulls them off Rachel's face, so she can use them to cover her own bloodshot eyes.

"I have a headache."

"Ha! You have a headache! Fuck my night—how bad I need to pee right now is giving me a headache."

"Don't they have toilets in the cells?"

"If you mean a hole filled with orange peels and diarrhea with a metal rim covered in puke, then yeah." Sadie presses the button in the elevator. "And stop looking so fucking awake, you're pissing me off even more."

"Did you get any sleep?"

"Yeah right, lay down on that nasty mat and risk head lice—as if! I was lucky enough—if you can call it that—to get my own cell. I could have been thrown in the cage with the crackhead prostitutes and piss-covered homeless people. But they still took the underwire out of my push-up bra. Do I look like the type of person to pick a lock or shiv a whore with a bra wire!?"

"Right now?"

"That was my favorite bra, too—bye bye fifty-dollar good sex."

"I was with a friend when you called, so I had to bring her with."

"What!? You don't have any friends besides me. It better not be one of those stupid strippers who kisses your ass for discounts at the sex den."

"It's a chick I met through Justin. She's one of his friends."

"Are you freaking kidding me? I look like this and I have to walk outside and be all nice to some random bitch? Whatever—I can't make any promises."

"Whatever."

The elevator opens to the main floor and Sadie hesitates to exit. "Shit," she hisses.

"What now?"

"I don't want to meet anyone looking like this."

"She's not gonna care."

A security guard approaches the elevator.

"Come on," Rachel says. "You're making a scene."

Sadie folds her arms.

"You know most people would be more concerned about meeting someone new just after being released from jail, but hey—hair is important too."

"Fuck jail."

Cerise is pacing out front and waves. Dark clouds had rolled in and shadowed the block while Rachel was inside.

Sadie smoothes her wrinkled gray blouse.

Rachel starts introductions but is interrupted by Sadie screaming.

"What the fuck is she doing here!?" Sadie throws a large plastic zip-lock bag (holding the contents of her purse) at Cerise.

Cerise ducks. "Holy shit! Do I know you?"

Sadie stomps her feet. "This is the worst day of my life!" Sadie grabs Rachel's arm and digs her nails into her flesh, dragging her across the concrete away from Cerise.

"That's the bitch in the purple wig," she says.

"What?"

"The skank who Eric ditched me to fuck at that party the other night—that's her!"

"That chick was wearing a wig. She could have been anyone."

"That's her, Rachel. I'm not a fucking idiot. I don't get so wasted I can't even remember people—like *she* obviously does!"

"Maybe because that's *not* her!"

Sadie folds her arms and looks down.

"Fine, let's say that *is* her. What are you gonna do about it? You aren't married to Eric. He isn't even your boyfriend. He was just some dumbass from work who you were fucking until something better came along. You're probably more pissed that you weren't in the threesome than that you got ditched for it. And she obviously had no idea he was with you. This is Eric's fault, not hers. Plus, I don't think that's her anyway."

Rachel hopes Cerise wasn't the girl in the purple wig. It would make her think she's just a pit stop on the way to the next distraction for Cerise. She's also grossed out by the aphorism that having sex with someone means you also had sex with all their previous partners. This is especially disturbing when Rachel remembers the guy with the lazy eye who always smelled like Funions that Sadie pity fucked last summer. But Sadie has a history of sabotaging new friendships for Rachel and can't be trusted.

"Why are you so hell bent on defending this chick? Who the fuck is she to you?"

"I just don't want to look like an asshole to Justin."

"Fine. I'll keep it together for *you*, but he better be awesome in bed because this bitch deserves to get her ass whooped. She's lucky I want to go home and delouse myself so bad I could cry. Maybe I got lucky and did get lice and I can just sit real close to her in the car."

Cerise walks up with a cigarette in her mouth that she's attempting to light. "Everything okay?" she asks through pursed lips.

"Whatever—let's just go." Sadie storms off toward the parking lot, pausing to pick up her empty purse and baggie of possessions.

"She's pleasant," Cerise says, taking a long drag off her cigarette.

Rachel starts the car and watches Sadie through the rearview angrily dumping the contents of the plastic bag back into her gray and white checkered pleather purse. "So, what the hell happened?"

"I got into a fight with the cashier at the pet shop in the mall. The puppies looked hungry. I asked if they'd been fed and she went maniacal, like some kind of mental patient."

"That's all you said?" Rachel asks.

"Okay—fine, she might have also been a chick from high school who used to call me a slut. And I might have called her a stupid bitch before I pushed her off her feet, and then she jumped up and chased me out of the store into the food court with a broom, so I ripped it out of her hand and tripped her with it. I could have gotten away from security if there hadn't been so many damn kids in line for the carousel...and if I wasn't wearing these stupid flops."

"You hate the mall."

"Mom's Appliance Munchhausen is out of control again and she sent me to Sears to look at some refrigerator with a separate compartment to keep milk colder than everything else."

Cerise turns around to face Sadie in the backseat. "What's Appliance Munchhausen?"

Sadie sighs. "Can you please explain it to *your friend*, Rachel."

"Munchhausen by Proxy—when a parent purposely makes their kid sick, so they need a lot of attention. Sadie's mom sabotages her appliances, so she can get new ones. Every time one of her friends or neighbors gets something better than her, she does it. It's the only way she can get Sadie's dad to dole out the cash for new stuff. We busted her severing wires behind the oven one day, so we call it Appliance Munchhausen."

Cerise laughs. "That's some sick shit."

"Hey—don't judge! Your dad probably dances around the living room in your underwear and fucks vases."

Cerise turns back around to face Sadie. "My dad is dead."

Sadie looks stunned. "Shit—I'm sorry."

Cerise laughs. "Kidding!"

"Ahhh! I swear to gawd, Rachel, I'm gonna kick this bitch's ass." Sadie throws the purse off her lap, unbuckles her seat belt and starts climbing over the seat.

Rachel pulls into the McDonald's parking lot across the street from the jail and slams on the brake throwing Sadie backward. "Go pee!"

Sadie shakes it off and gets out of the car, cursing the whole way inside. Rachel parks, then drops her head and rubs her temples. "Do you own a purple wig?" she asks Cerise.

"I have lots of wigs."

"Yeah, but do you have a purple one?"

"Why, do you want to wear it and get freaky?"

"Please—."

"Fine, Rachel, yeah—I have a purple wig. Why the hell does it matter?" Cerise seems confused until a sense of knowing blankets her face and she turns to look out the window. "Look, I don't like myself very much lately, but if you start seeing me the way I see myself I don't think I can handle it."

"I don't want to be someone you're just *killing time* with."

Cerise's eyes well up and she grabs Rachel's hand. "I would never do that to you."

So much emotion is coming from Cerise, Rachel feels drained. Cerise kisses her and Rachel forgets everything until something cold and pointy smacks her in the face. She pulls back dazed and sees a ketchup packet lying in her lap.

"I knew you were trying to steal my best friend—you fucking skank! Eric wasn't enough, huh!?" Sadie lunges over Rachel through the open window and tries to claw at Cerise.

Cerise jumps out of the car and Rachel pushes Sadie back, screaming for her to calm down.

Sadie backs off long enough to take aim and throw half a cheeseburger at Cerise, then screams at Rachel, "I don't give a shit if you want to switch teams—just don't do it with her! You deserve better, Rachel." Sadie waits for Cerise to retaliate and fuel extra incentive to beat her down.

Cerise just stands there looking defeated. "Yeah, she probably does."

"Don't think you can play the humble-card and not still get your ass kicked," Sadie says.

"Look, I didn't know that guy was your boyfriend. I have no idea who you are. And I'm sorry you hate me so much, but if you want to spend the rest of the weekend in jail, then by all means, let's go ape-shit on each other right here, right now."

"You know what—I'm done with this bullshit. It's me or her, Rachel."

"C'mon," Rachel says. "Do we really have to do this?"

Sadie puts her hands on her hips and waits.

Cerise leans against Rachel's car with her arms folded and head bowed, as if knowing she's about to be booted from Rachel's life.

Finding out Cerise was the girl in the purple wig hurts, but it was the same night Rachel was fucking Justin. And even though having sex with random strangers while intoxicated is a different kind of lonely, Sadie might as well be looking into a mirror while yelling at Cerise. Rachel realizes Sadie's not mad about Eric, she's mad about Cerise stealing Rachel, and demanding that Rachel choose a side is just another one of her selfish games. "Sorry, Sadie—I'm not playing."

"I didn't give you a *choice*."

"Fuck You," Rachel says.

Sadie walks up to Cerise, who backs up and prepares for a blow. "Give me my fucking sweatshirt!" she yells.

"What?"

Sadie points to the navy-blue hoodie with a white hibiscus

design that Cerise is wearing. "I gave that sweatshirt to Rachel."

"For gawds sake, Sadie—what are we, in junior high now?" Rachel says.

Cerise shrugs, pulls the sweatshirt over her head and hands it to Sadie, who then grabs her purse out of the backseat and walks away.

Cerise stands in the parking lot wearing nothing but low-rise, faded jeans and a black lace bra. Her cocoa skin is covered in small white goosebumps. In a situation where most girls might look defeated, Cerise appears triumphant as two teenage boys whistle, and a gawking man nods and smiles before being punched in the shoulder by his wife. Rachel takes her jacket off and hands it to Cerise.

"Should we follow?" Cerise asks.

"She'll probably just stomp around the block a few times then come back."

"I'm really sorry."

Rachel shrugs. The river of serotonin that the pink pill had rained into her brain nearly twenty-four hours earlier, creating the happiest version of herself she's ever experienced, is now completely dried up. Finding something to make her feel better is like searching for potable water in the Atacama Desert. Rachel has never been suicidal, but she's sure this is what it must feel like. She used to think people who committed suicide were selfish because, ultimately, they end all their pain and leave behind a wake of suffering loved ones, but if this is how they feel, she has a completely new depth of empathy for their anguish.

"You coming down?" Cerise asks.

Rachel turns on the radio.

"The cigarettes pick me back up." She digs the pack out of her purse and lights up. "Oh, yeah—sorry," she says, and gets out of the car.

Rachel slumps down in the seat and watches five fat crows in the parking lot feverishly gorge on discarded French-fries. Yet a raspberry bush full of berries grows only a few feet away. I'm like those crows', she thinks. *I gorge myself on the discarded, never holding out for what's healthy.*

One hour later, still no sign of Sadie. Cerise is silent for most of the ride home. They kiss briefly when Rachel drops her off. And for the first time in two days, Rachel realizes how much Cerise tastes like an ashtray.

Rachel is standing alone on a dark-pebble lakeshore surrounded in western white pines. A purple, red, and orange sunset reflects off the choppy surface of the water, painting the lake a more spectacular myriad of colors than the sky. In the distance, a girl wearing a long black dress is peering over the edge of a wood dock that extends into the lake. Her thick, sandy-brown curls are motionless, but as Rachel approaches, she can hear the heavy dress rustling in the wind. Just as she gets close enough to reach out and touch her, the girl steps off of the dock. Rachel lunges to grab her but misses. The girl sinks—never struggling. Despite having no idea who she is, Rachel feels a tremendous loss and jumps in. The water is dark and murky, and no matter how hard Rachel swims, she can't resurface. Her chest is heavy, and just when she thinks she's about to drown, she wakes up gasping for air. Ewoka falls sideways off of Rachel's chest. She looks down and sees the girl from the dream standing at the foot of the bed. She has large dark circles under her eyes and is soaking wet with clumps of matted hair hanging over her shoulders. She looks like Cerise. Rachel screams. The image fades and she's alone again, panting and crying.

The only other time she had seen someone she knew outside of a dream was just before her Grandmother had died. The burden of what the dream forebodes feels like being smacked in the head by a shoe in flight during a concert. One hour, two cookies, and a long conversation with Ewoka later, she decides that drug-induced dreams shouldn't be taken seriously.

Her phone is beeping in the pocket of her jeans lying on the bathroom floor. Two missed calls from Justin and another apologetic text from Cerise. It's still early, so she returns Justin's call. He sounds relieved to hear from her and the pleasant conversation persuades her to meet him for dinner the following night.

Ambush

Tanzi's car is parked just a few spaces away from Rachel in the parking lot of the restaurant Justin had suggested near Pier 66. He hops out to meet Rachel. They hug, and she does an awkward vertical head maneuver to avoid kissing. He seems to shake it off quickly.

"I'm really glad you came," he says. His phone rings. He looks annoyed and presses *ignore*.

The minimal conversation they do have is flat, and he fiddles with the silverware while ordering, staring at her intently during salads, making the already awkward situation that much worse. She didn't anticipate how bad she would feel when she saw him. Hadn't he been the one to say they should *see other people*? Doesn't that exonerate her of any wrongdoing? Sure, hooking up with his friend's ex-girlfriend was inconsiderate, but was it a crime? In relationship court, she would probably be acquitted, but the fact that it would need to go to court makes her feel guilty. She considers confessing but can't think of any good that will come of it. Worst-case scenario, he gets angry and storms out, leaving her with the bill. Best case, he acts like it's no big deal, but then she's left thinking that he doesn't really care about her or is somehow absolved of guilt for whatever *he's been doing* for the last few days. Either way, thinking about it is getting on her nerves. She spent her entire childhood seeking the forgiveness of men for her *alleged* sins and she refuses to adhere to those rules anymore. In fact, the more she thinks about it, the less guilty she feels and almost wants to rub it in his face. Instead, she takes a deep breath and realizes that she does not owe him anything and should just keep her mouth shut. She eats in silence, hoping something will explode in the kitchen, forcing everyone to evacuate.

Halfway through her grilled salmon, a large man at a candle-lit table near a wall of windows overlooking the water proposes to his girlfriend. A blonde with a tight perm who looks like she's pushing forty and is desperately in need of a sperm donor, screams, *"Yes!"* The entire lower level breaks into applause. Justin laughs nervously and runs his fingers through his hair.

"Look," he says. "I admit that whole scene the other morning was pretty callous. These last few days spent wondering what you've been doing and realizing I took you for granted, have made me feel like total shit. You're awesome; you always make me feel better about everything. I know I can't take it back but could we like start over or something because I would really like the chance to show you I'm not the kind of guy to disappear at the first sign of trouble—and I don't need the option to see other people."

Shit, shit, shit. Rachel smiles. She thought she was coming to a let's-be-friends dinner. The swank location should have tipped her off. She's off her anticipatory game and flounders for an appropriate reaction. She pretends to chew far longer than is necessary and pauses for a couple extra gulps of water. "I'm sorry, too. I came at you with no willingness to compromise and I didn't put a lot of thought into the stress you're dealing with. I've put some thought into it now and I actually think you may have been right."

Justin sits back in his chair and folds his arms. He seems confused, as if trying to decide whether her response is a test or not. "Am I missing something?"

"Don't get me wrong; I'm not saying we're gonna start fucking with no strings attached. I expect the occasional call to know you're still alive. But if you're busy, texting to tell me I'm fabulous will suffice. Just don't show up in the middle of the night all horny. I don't do the booty-call thing."

He seems relieved and maybe even a little amused. Turned-on for sure. The spark she'd seen when he first started coming over to the porn shop to talk is reignited and she likes it. His apology pressed the reset button, and as complicated as everything just became, she's glad. She knows he's better for her than Cerise, but he's not ready to commit and she's not ready to let Cerise go.

He follows her to her car and lingers for a kiss. Against her better judgment, she gives in—like a good faith gesture to prove she's invested in the reconciliation attempt and not just trying to end dinner on a positive note. But she forgot how tender his kiss is and it's hard to stop.

"Sure you don't want me to spend the night?" he asks.

She does. Practically the only time she gets a full night sleep is when someone spends the night. She's gone such long stretches alone, enduring so many rough nights, she hates the idea of passing up his company. But whoring herself out for a full night sleep doesn't feel right. She declines and doesn't get much resistance because his phone won't stop ringing. She waves a final goodbye. Driving home in silence, she resumes wondering how guilty she should feel.

Rachel rounds the corner to her apartment and finds Cerise sitting against the door holding an empty beer bottle. Her skin is mustard-yellow in the porch light and the rings under her eyes are a faint greenish hue. "Where the hell have you been?" Cerise asks.

"I wasn't aware we were on an inform-you-of-my-every-move basis."

"Yeah, well—not calling me back for two days is a while—don't ya think."

"We were together yesterday morning."

"You never called last night to let me know everything was okay, and you never called me today—that's *two* days." Cerise stands and stumbles around, barely able to hold herself up.

Rachel shakes her head.

"Oh, you don't think you have to take me seriously cuz I'm drunk? Well, I'm not! I've only had a few. Where have you been?"

Rachel holds up a small blue bag. "Shopping for a nightlight."

"For four hours!" Cerise turns and chucks the beer bottle into the wooded area beyond the manicured grass. The bottle bounces off a tree then clinks on a rock.

Rachel opens the door and pulls Cerise inside. "What are you doing here?"

"Just *killing time.*"

"Why are you wasted after the speech yesterday about getting sober?"

"How about youuuuu tell me where you've been for so long."

"I met Justin for dinner."

"There ya go—*that's* why I'm wasted!"

"That's shit! You had no idea where I was. What if I'd been at church or something—then what's your excuse?"

Cerise throws herself down on the couch. "Don't need one, cuz that's *not* where you were!"

"Whatever."

"Whatever, whatever, whatever," Cerise repeats in a singsong voice, waving her index fingers as if directing a choir. She reaches around her back and pulls a book out of her jeans throwing it at Rachel. Nabokov's *Lolita* smacks Rachel in the stomach and falls to the floor.

"You're fucking crazy!"

"Don't call me crazy!" Cerise screams as she leans forward, pounding her fists on the front of the couch. Her cheeks are flushed, and her shirt is cut so low that her breasts—stuffed into a bra that's obviously too small—are about to burst out the top.

"You need to calm the hell down."

Cerise stands up and storms across the room stopping an inch from Rachel's face. "No—I *need* you not to be such a fucking liar! *Oh, Cerise, bring me your worst—I can take it*," she says.

"That was about headaches, withdrawal anguish, and bad moods that make you annoyed by unusual things like yoga instructors and puppets. I'm not willing to be your drunken punching bag!"

"I don't want to punch you. I want to love you. Why don't you love me?" Cerise yells, pushing Rachel against the wall and kissing her.

Her lips tremble and Rachel can feel Cerise's entire body shaking. She pushes her away. "Hell no—get out!"

Cerise stumbles backward, falling into the pile of blankets that had been padding for Pink-stripe and Plaid's hookup the other night. She pounds her fists into the blankets and laughs hysterically. Kicking her legs up in the air, she sends a shoe flying across the room.

It's like watching a two-year-old throw a temper tantrum. Rachel doesn't think she's ever seen anything like it from an adult. She's no longer mad; she just pities Cerise.

"I'm going to kill myself to show you all!" Cerise yells.

"I don't know many people who would miss *this*. How about you give people something to miss, *and then* shove it in their face. When was the last time you thought about someone other than yourself for an extended period of time? Maybe if you pulled your head out of your own ass for five minutes you wouldn't have to drown yourself in drugs and alcohol to cope with the stench of life."

Cerise's mouth is gaping.

"The only thing that makes you ever consider suicide is the downer from the rainbow array of pills you pop."

"You don't know shit. You live here by yourself with your stupid cat."

"At least I'm sober!"

Cerise flips her off and lies back, then starts passing out.

Rachel holds out her hand. "Come on, I'll take you home."

"I can't go home. They'll lock me up in that place again with the fat-headed doctor and his bitchy minions."

"Then maybe you should stop stomping your feet and using suicide threats to manipulate people into letting you do whatever you want."

Cerise giggles. "How about we go in the bedroom and I'll make *you* do whatever I want?"

"The last place I'm going with you is the bedroom."

"Well, I'm going wherever you're going."

Rachel sighs. "That's good because I'm going to your house."

"Because you love me?"

"Yes, Cerise, I love you." Rachel leans down and puts Cerise's shoe back on, then leads her out to the car. Cerise is quiet or asleep for most of the ride home. Rachel counts twenty-seven traffic lights and feels lucky that only five are red because at almost every stop Cerise says, "Thanks for the ride," then tries to get out. When they finally reach her house, she's completely passed-out. Rachel leans across her and opens the door. Cerise wakes up, mumbles, "Thanks," and pulls a crumpled piece of paper out of her pocket, hands it to Rachel, then stumbles up the cracked, uneven walkway and disappears inside. Rachel opens the waded ball and finds Justin's number scribbled at least a hundred times.

Tattooed
Prince Charming

*R*achel pulls up to the address on Pac-Man's business card, squinting to read the black and orange hours sign:

9:00 – 6:00

Mon – Sat

She flicks the shiny white card, debating whether she really wants to go inside. *Sorry* scribbled on the back is at an angle that makes her wonder if he's left-handed. This is probably the last place she should be. But the capriciousness of her present relationships compels her to investigate whether the attraction she felt the other night was genuine or just pink-pill induced. Both of the bay doors are closed. No one has seen her yet, so she could easily drive away, and he would never know. But the same compulsion that drove her here insists she go inside.

The door beeps as she enters a small customer service

area with what used to be a white linoleum floor, turned tan from years of infrequent mopping—if ever. The room smells of exhaust and gasoline. An artificial, faded ficus tree stands next to a laminate popup table holding an old, stained coffee machine. Against the far wall is a faded-green couch and a quarter machine filled with crumbled bits of candy coating. Above the couch is a crooked, framed poster of a red Ferrari parked on a beach.

A short, dark-skinned man with thick black hair, graying in large chunks near the front of his scalp, walks through an open door behind the table that Rachel assumes leads to the garage. He wipes greasy hands on the front of his faded gray coveralls. "Can I help you?"

"I'm looking for Evan," Rachel says.

The man looks her up and down. He nods then disappears.

Moments later, Evan appears.

She holds up the business card. "Someone left me a coupon for a free squeaky belt repair."

He smiles. "I'm glad you came. My dad didn't give you any shit, did he?"

"The mime I just talked to?"

"Only other guy here today."

The man pokes his head through the doorway. "No, I didn't embarrass you."

Rachel laughs. "He speaks."

The man nods and holds out his hand to shake. His smile accentuates leather crows-feet around the translucent blue eyes that his son had inherited. "His mother isn't around anymore to keep me in line, so he's always worried about what's gonna come out of this old man's mouth."

Rachel smiles. "Don't hold back. I need all the dirt I can get to keep *him* in line."

Evan's dad winks and elbows him in the side, then disappears again.

"Your dad seems nice."

"Yeah, but you can't get away with much working for your dad."

"I heard that!" his dad yells from the back.

Evan points to the front door. "Shall we?"

He knocks on the hood of the Charger. "Pop-'er open— please."

Rachel hesitates to find the latch.

He folds his arms and shakes his head.

She's frustrated—she knows exactly where the latch is, he just makes her nervous. She finally pops the hood and curses herself. He tells her to start it up, listens to what sounds like a frantic bat trapped inside the engine, looks around, then gives her the cue to shut it down. He holds up one finger and runs back inside. He comes back with a ratchet, does something she can't see from the driver's seat and tells her to start it back up. Silence. He pokes his head around the side and smiles.

"Yay!" Rachel claps.

"Easy fix," he says, closing the hood.

"I really appreciate it."

"Now I need you to do something for me," he says.

"I thought fixing my car was to apologize for messing with my head the other night."

"Nah—that's what the note on the business card was for. I just fixed your car cuz I think you're cool. For tightening the belt, I think you should go out with me this weekend."

Rachel gets that excited feeling in her stomach, like finally reaching the top of the water slide and having to barrel down blind, hoping she won't run into anyone stuck in the tube— apprehensive, but excited the whole way. "I think I can do that, but I'm gonna need one more small favor first."

Evan leans against the front of her car.

"Do you remember where my apartment is?"

"Pretty much."

She pulls a piece of paper out of her purse and scribbles the address. "Just show up after you get off work tonight. Oh—and wear dark clothes."

"You're not like a professional thief or something are you?"

Rachel laughs.

He smirks. "I'll be there."

"Bring the ratchet!"

Rachel isn't entirely sure what she's doing. Juggling this much sex is ambitious, even for her. Part of her had hoped she'd see Evan and he'd be a jerk and that would be the end of it. Now she's worried and excited, mostly worried. She's especially concerned that everyone involved has too much contact with each other. This type of situation always seems easier when no one knows the other exists. Rachel fantasizes about them ganging up and making a pact to ostracize her as punishment. She pictures Justin fucking Cerise and Cerise fucking Evan, then Evan and Justin fighting and Cerise fucking them both at the same time as consolation. The daymare gets completely out of control when somehow her ninth grade English teacher (also Justin's teacher) reprimands her for being promiscuous. And just when she's about to change her name and leave town, she realizes she passed the entrance to the sandwich shop where she wanted to stop for lunch. She takes a deep breath and promises herself she won't let it get that out of control—even if she has to painfully eliminate someone.

Evan shows up right on time, looking a bit nervous. "Okay, I'm here, but you're gonna have to do some explaining before I put my ass on the line."

Rachel nods, grabs his arm, and pulls him out of the apartment. He follows her across the parking lot and out onto the curb. "See that sign?" She points to a yellow diamond about twenty feet away that says SPEED HUMP.

"Yeah."

"We're gonna steal it."

He laughs. "Is this some kinda new-guy initiation?"

"I wanna give it to a friend for her birthday."

"Sure, yeah—who needs all the shiny stuff at the mall when you can steal a street sign?"

"Exactly!"

"Man, I knew I was gonna regret that stupid *I'm gay* thing." He walks up to the sign, eyeballs the bolts, heads back into the apartment, picks out a couple of sockets and hands them to Rachel. "Do you know how to use a ratchet?"

"Urg—yes."

He shrugs. "Shit, you never know."

They see car lights and run behind a bush. Evan says,

"I think you might owe me two dates after this stunt." He kneels down on the road next to the sign and tells Rachel to climb on his shoulders. "I'm gonna hoist you up to remove the bolts." Three stops to jump down and hide in the bushes later, the sign finally comes down. Evan hauls the flat hunk of metal—considerably larger than it appeared while passing by in a moving vehicle—into Rachel's apartment. It stands about the height of the couch and is almost half as wide.

Rachel smiles and cheers their success. "Now all you have to do is tell me why you said you were gay."

"I didn't want to hook up with you on X. I really like you, and you can't start a meaningful relationship with freaky drug sex cuz it's all downhill from there. Plus, Cerise seemed to have dibs on you—and if that's what you wanted, I didn't want to interfere."

"Do you do a lot of drugs?" Rachel asks.

"Nah, I'm not really into that scene. I don't even know why I did it last weekend. I've just been in a weird place lately and I guess I needed to get outside myself. Funny, to go deeper in to get out, but it worked. And I met you, which so far, has made me look like a liar, and resulted in my breaking at least three laws, so things are looking up already."

Rachel laughs.

"So, do you *do* Cerise a lot?" he asks.

Rachel is stunned. "No," she finally says.

"Good. Well, I gotta go, but I'll see you this weekend." He knocks on the sign, laughs, and gives her a thumbs-up as he walks out the door.

Out of Order

It was one of those moments like opening the door to a magazine salesperson or Jehovah's Witness. After which, you spend the rest of the day thinking about everything you could have accomplished if you had that hour of your life back. Not that any of those things would have *actually* been accomplished, but the notion of the loss is enough to trigger the *what was I thinking* moment.

This time it was an unknown number that duped Rachel into answering. But it wasn't the five minutes of conversation time she wanted back; it was the sixteen years of childhood that the person attached to the voice on the other end of the line had stolen. Well, to be fair, twelve years—she can't really remember the first four.

"I heard you might have some free time to meet for lunch while I'm in town," her dad says with a labored tone, as if returning a call to the morgue—*Yes, I will be there at five to identify the body.*

Rachel laughs. "Nope, I'm booked this week."

"Okay then, sorry to bother you." He sounds surprisingly disappointed.

"I'm kidding."

"Oh, yeah—ha—good one," he says.

They agree on a place and time that afternoon, which Rachel changes to thirty-minutes later at the last second, so she has time to dispose of the illegally acquired city property covered with a sheet in the backseat of her car. He would not find it humorous and might even consider turning her in for stealing. She is yet to meet another compulsive liar with as austere principles as her father.

Rachel parks a few houses down from Sadie's parents, and then lugs the huge SPEED HUMP sign up the driveway. She sets it on the doorstep with a note that says, "A tribute to our fabulousness," rings the doorbell, then runs—sure she's going to be caught, but isn't. After two passes around the block, the sign is gone.

Rachel sits in her car outside the pizza place where she had agreed to meet her dad. She assesses the godliness of her appearance—no cleavage, no offensive language on her t-shirt, earrings in only one pair of her three sets of holes, no visible tattoos, and not much makeup. The only incriminating evidence is a cigarette that Cerise must have dropped. Rachel chucks it out the window, then sees her dad inside, sitting at a table in the corner. He looks very official in his dark-gray business suit, like an IRS agent come to audit her.

She hasn't seen him in nearly five years. He's thicker and his light brown hair is thinner and grayer than she remembered. His presence is disorienting. Like the kid's game where you're supposed to pick out the item that doesn't belong, he's a broccoli floret in a row of fruit. He's invading her comfort zone, judging every block within five-miles of her address. No doubt searching out dilapidated buildings to report back to her stepmother as proof of the squalor she's forced to live in as punishment for turning her back on their god. Fortunately, the only rundown building nearby is an old gas station that was torn down months ago. Now a clean lot of raked dirt sits empty with a white *for sale* sign.

It's late in the afternoon for lunch, and even though the tinted windows and dim, low-hanging lights create a late evening ambiance, it's still too early for dinner, so the restaurant is quiet. Besides the woman and her son sitting with a pile of wadded napkins next to a half-empty pizza pan, only one other man is in a booth in the far corner. He's filling out paperwork, and on second glance, seems to be the manager tallying time cards.

Rachel smiles as she approaches her dad. He looks nervous and stands as if preparing for a hug but hangs back and bows his head like a formal greeting between Asian colleagues. Rachel thinks *fuck it* and leans in for a hug. He reciprocates but resists with locked-elbows and a boxlike embrace. He sits back down and asks how close she lives to where they are, then cracks a couple of dry jokes about root-*beer.*

Rachel responds with the most genuine pity laugh she can muster.

It reminds her of the days when he would do Bert and Ernie impersonations to entertain her while her stepmother was gone doing egg-carton craft projects at church with like-minded, obtuse women suffering from what Rachel views as a form of Stockholm syndrome and an underdeveloped sense of purpose. His eyes squint almost closed when he laughs, just like hers—the same hazel (mostly green) eyes, but his are now framed in a red spider web and the colors have dulled. He keeps the conversation light until she orders. Then, likely settled into the comfort of knowing she'll be trapped for at least the next forty-five minutes, he says, "I hear you're dating a Mexican. How's that working out?"

"Great. He's just about convinced me to quit my job and become a drug mule."

"You know, I'm not as narrow-minded as you think. Our church is the fastest growing church in Mexico, so they must be pretty smart people."

"Yeah, well, faith is easier to sell to people who live in shacks framed by milk crates. I just hope the church is giving them some kind of discount on the gold-leafed statues atop their new temples."

He shifts in his seat and takes a large bite of an oily breadstick. Rachel is shocked to see a level of restraint he had never exhibited when she was young. Ten years ago, she would have been running to her bedroom, desperately trying to hold the door shut while he pounded his way in to show her what it feels like to disagree with dad. "Well, quitting your job sounds like a nice idea, at least."

Rachel laughs. If and when she stops working at the porn shop, her parents will be the last to know.

He reaches into his interior suit jacket pocket and pulls out a folded manila envelope. "I have something for you that I've been holding onto against your mother's wishes."

Rachel cringes. As if referring to *that woman* as her mother isn't bad enough, if her father were a stuffed doll with a pull string, *against your mother's wishes* would be track three.

"She wants to be your friend, you know. I hope that giving you this will open a door for reconciliation."

"You have to have been friends at some point to reconcile, *Dad*. She's not well. She doesn't like me, she doesn't know me, and if she's ever tried it was just a performance for you."

"She just thought being a mother would be different, I guess. She wasn't emotionally prepared for the spirited, four-year-old baggage that came with marrying me." He bows his head and slides the envelope across the table. "You don't have to open it now."

His face is so serious the envelope might as well contain the date Rachel is going to die. She's angry. He's put her in a precarious situation in a public place, somewhere cold and isolated from true emotional reaction. If whatever the envelope contains is as grave as the look on his face, a pizza parlor is *not* an appropriate venue.

The server—not much younger than Rachel—is a brunette with her hair pulled back in a ponytail, wearing a red, rumpled apron. She approaches the table, sees Rachel's face and turns back around without saying a word.

Opening the envelope, Rachel pulls out a few papers and a stack of photographs. On top is one from her father and Emily's wedding day that she'd never seen before. She stares at the yellowed photo of her *real* mother wearing a simple, pale pink, ruffled dress with her hair tied back in a ribbon, and her father with feathered hair wearing a white suit. "Pretty snazzy," Rachel says, holding it up.

He chuckles. "That was a good year for fashion."

Rachel thumbs through the contents of the envelope and looks closer at the photos. Some are her newborn baby pictures that she'd never seen. In most, she's a year or two old, hiding in empty drawers and laundry hampers, always peeking out with a huge smile. The only constant besides Rachel is Emily holding her or smiling in the background of every photo. Rachel thumbs through the stack and finds the title for her car, then unfolds a death certificate from the Costa Rican Civil Registry.

Coughing out words while choking on a sip of water, he says, "We received that...a few...months ago."

When Rachel was nine or ten years old, she had spent three weeks in the backyard practicing for field day at school. She was determined to do the football toss. She couldn't jump very far, and she couldn't hang from the monkey bars for very long, but she liked football because it was a way to get her dad's attention. She got so good at throwing a spiral—for a kid—that her dad told her she might actually win. Up until that moment, she had never thought about winning. She just enjoyed the time with her father, which turns out to be entirely different from what her father had in mind. Trying is accomplished by simply participating. Winning is daunting because the only alternative is losing, which comes with a completely new set of disappointments that Rachel wasn't ready to deal with, especially from him. For all she knew, he could disappear as easily as Emily had, so Rachel was terrified of disappointing him.

When field day finally came, she got so sick to her stomach, she couldn't even try. She spent the afternoon sitting at a desk with her head down in a dark classroom. Later she found out there were no winners. Everyone came back to class with ribbons, candy, silly prizes, and funny stories just for participating. She spent years chastising herself for never trying and vowed not to be that person ever again. Finding out her parents had kept Emily's death from her isn't shocking; finding out she's been left sitting alone in the dark again by the only person in her family who hadn't treated her like a leper, destroys her motivation to maintain civility with any of them.

Rachel leaves her dad sitting at the table and walks into the bathroom. The first stall is locked. *Out of Order* is scribbled in black marker on a white piece of paper taped to the scratched red door that won't close. She goes into the only stall with a working door latch and locks herself inside. Fortunately, she doesn't need to use the toilet because the contents of the bowl are as foul as her day. Her phone rings. She pulls it out of her pocket to switch to silent. Cerise. Rachel presses *ignore*, then scrolls through the stack of Cerise's text message rants, beginning as belligerent rationalizations that evolve into apologies and pleas for reconciliation. Her phone rings again.

She flinches, dropping the phone into the toilet. It's only visible for a few seconds before disappearing beneath a pile of egesta sludge. Rachel gasps as she watches Cerise sink into the murky depths for the second time that week, but this time she has no desire to jump in and save her.

Eventually, Rachel marches back to the table and gathers her jacket, purse, and contents of the envelope. Five more minutes and she won't have a choice about quitting her job.

"I'm sorry," her dad says.

Rachel flips him off and walks out.

"The way I see it,
if you want the rainbow,
you gotta put up with the rain."
–Dolly Parton

Rachel wakes the next morning groggy, clutching the photograph of the rainbow with the quote about rain scribbled on the back that Emily had sent from Costa Rica last Christmas.

Living all over the United States had taught Rachel a lot about rain. Sadie reminds Rachel of Southwest rain that's hard and dry, evaporating almost as soon as it hits the ground. When it fights back against the scorching sun it comes in torrents, flooding the arroyos. It's streaked by long flashing bolts of purple, teal, and white lightning, as if putting a signature on its vengeance. Proud rain.

Cerise reminds Rachel of Southeast rain—the wettest and heaviest of all rains. It's like the water vapor normally suspended in humid air collects and expands to the size of almonds, enveloping everything while ocean waves swell then slither through towns, leaving snake-like rivers of destruction, followed by gale-force winds that prune the limbs from trees weakened by the storm. Apocalyptic rain.

Justin reminds Rachel of Northwest rain. Still and silent. Difficult to see where one drop ends and the next begins, mirroring the transformation of blue sky to an endless slab of concrete-gray. The rain is so thin and silent you often don't realize it's raining until soggy pant hems stick to your ankles and chill your legs. Tranquil rain.

Rachel's father reminds her of Midwest rain. Large and loud. It falls from black and gray storybook clouds that form when the villain's arms are raised. It's accompanied by rolling thunder and bursts of light that illuminate the entire moss-green sky, swiftly cleansing large leaves and tree houses, while stirring up the mineral-rich aerosol just below the turf. Purging rain.

Emily was the breeze that guides the clouds and portends the coming storm—exhilarating.

Sea Stars

*O*n the rare occasion that thunder is actually heard in Seattle, Rachel gets excited. Today is one of those days. Her window rattles. Ewoka jumps on the bed, burrowing beneath the blanket. Rachel tries to console her but knows the next rumble will make her efforts futile, so she constructs a pillow fort for Ewoka, then gets out of bed to begin her day. It's the first morning in three days that she woke up feeling okay since seeing her dad and finding out about Emily's death. She makes it through breakfast without an urge to cry or punch the wall.

For a few hours, she just lies on the couch, listening to mellow music while watching storm clouds float away, exposing the clear sky. Ewoka is curled up in a ball just above her head on the back of the sofa cushion. Just as Rachel is about to fall asleep, a bright glare from sun beaming through the kitchen window reflects off a steel pan full of petrified tomato soup that's balanced atop a stack of four-day-old dishes, causing her to suddenly feel very awake. She decides to go for walk.

Layered in a purple Down vest over a long sleeved, black fleece sweater and chunky-knit hat with matching gloves, she wanders the neighborhood. The parted clouds expose a spectrum of violet and blue sky with wisps of pink in the horizon. She passes the small, stationary dock near her apartment—commonly congested with fisherman—but today it's empty. The waterlogged support beams have expanded, eliminating the gaps that usually make it easy to search for life below. She walks out to the end of the dock and leans over the edge looking for starfish suctioned to the beams, finding only a large cluster of spiky barnacles. She takes a long, deep breath to inhale the purifying scent of salt water—always stronger after a cleansing rain. Rachel checks her new phone for missed calls or messages. Evan had sent a text saying hello.

Moments after arriving back at her apartment, barely enough time to shove her gloves and hat in the rear of her sock drawer, someone knocks. Rachel isn't expecting anyone and hesitates to answer until she hears her dad yell, "I know you're in there. I saw you walk in."

Rachel opens the door. "That's kinda creepy."

"Yes, well, I'm sure *creepy* is the least of my offenses," he says, marching in with a tall brown box and three bags.

He's flushed after the hike from the parking lot with the load and she struggles to picture him running up and down football fields during his college days.

"I would have come yesterday," he says, pausing to catch his breath, "but I didn't know your address and it took me until today to get it from Mom because I forgot to pack my cell phone charger."

"What's all this?" She peeks in a bag.

"Tupperware," he says, chuckling. "Kidding—we both know women like you don't need stuff like that."

Oh boy, Rachel thinks, *here we go.*

"No, no, no—it's all good. Get that look off your face. Thing is, they're remodeling the second floor of the hotel where I've been staying. It's been so loud that they comp'd me for two nights. I almost sent the money to one of those families you're so concerned about living in a milk-crate house in Mexico, but I didn't come this far to leave things the way we did the other day." He puts his hands in the pockets of his dark slacks, jangles his keys, and glances around the apartment in a reserved way, as if trying to avoid seeing something he'll regret, eventually just fixating on the blank television screen. "I hope I bought the right stuff, and the right type of easel—that's what's in the big box, by the way." He points to the box—a nervous gesture. "Nice photo." He points at Seattle.

Rachel smiles.

"And maybe don't mention this to Mom. Your sister had to put off her ballet lessons for a couple of months already, and I'd rather not hear about it again for a while."

Rachel nods.

"Great, well, gotta fly—literally, my plane leaves in two hours."

As far back as Rachel can remember he'd been quick to

escape vulnerable situations, especially the kind that required any admonishment of guilt.

"The receipt is in one of the bags. Nice boy working at the art supply store down the road—not a single tattoo on him. You should go in there sometime—too much? Okay, I'm going now."

"Thanks, Dad."

He nods, pulling the door closed behind him.

The bags of art supplies and the boxed easel propped against the wall are the first presence anyone from her family has ever had in her Emerald City life. She makes a cucumber, sprouts, and avocado sandwich, eating while sitting next to the guilt-inspired pile of gifts. Hush money—intended to buy a moment of forgiveness because he won't emotionally invest any time in a meaningful resolve. Time invested being the only thing that could ever really lead to resolve, but it's a gesture nonetheless, more effort than he's made in years. Rachel rummages through the plastic sacks. Trace whiffs of her dad's spicy-citrus cologne dissipate as she attempts to assemble the easel while Ewoka bats at a tube of Phthalo-blue paint.

Dear Reader,

Time is precious, and I'm honored that you spent yours reading my work.

To celebrate the release of the second edition, I've included responses to the most common questions I received after the initial release of *The Light in the Sound*.

How Autobiographical is *The Light in the Sound?*

It's not. However, as my body of work goes, this will likely end up being the most autobiographical fiction I ever release. (There's a Gordian Knot for ya. Ha.) Like most authors, I was loosely inspired by life experience. I was raised by zealously religious parents. I left home at age 16. I worked in a porn shop when I was 18, and my first car was a Dodge Charger, though it certainly wasn't gifted to me. I busted my arse to buy it, and it was nowhere near as cool as the car Rachel drives. Beyond that, it's hit or miss throughout. ;)

Who Does Rachel End Up With?

Great question! But that was never the point. I consider this a love story, but not in the "conventional" sense. It's about her learning to love herself, mistakes and all. Rarely do people view us the way we view ourselves, and learning how to navigate those filters and love ourselves, despite the personas inflicted on us, is a message that's often overlooked in our society and is really what her love story is intended to be about: becoming comfortable in her own skin; not needing anyone else to "complete" her; developing the strength to stay open to finding a companion who loves and accepts her for her, flaws and all.

Will There Be A Sequel?

Never say never, but it's highly unlikely. I always intended this story to be a brief snapshot of a pivotal moment in someone's life that many of us can relate to—standing at a crossroads where we could so easily fall off the deep-end or rise up more confident than ever with greater self-awareness of one's inner strength to press forward with a replenished well of hope.

Following Rachel through nursing school or Seattle's art scene would feel too contrived. There are so many directions her life could go at this juncture, I think it's more fun leaving it open to reader speculation.

That said, there is a cut chapter from Rachel's story in my collection, *Neon and Flamingo*. It's a flashback to her early childhood that ended up feeling displaced and became a stand-alone "ghost" story. As difficult as "killing that darling" was, including it elsewhere as a puzzle piece for loyal readers was fun.

When Did You Decide to Become A Writer?

I didn't. It's always been a part of me, as much as my natural hair color or the freckles on the inside of my right knee that, when connected with pen lines, look like the little dipper. I knew the answer before I realized the question existed. I just wish my schedule were as singularly focused as my mind so I had time to produce more work. The plight of the working-class artist.

Onward to us all!

Acknowledgments

Deepest gratitude to my beloved husband, Josh Gonzales, for his unwavering encouragement and faith in me, as well as his enthusiastic willingness to cook *and clean* on nights I need to write.

Sincerest appreciation and thanks for the tireless efforts of my esteemed mentors who instilled confidence in my writing and championed this work from day one: TJ Rivard, Julie Brickman, and Philip F. Deaver.

Thank you to the workshop leaders and fellow writers who enthusiastically contributed valuable insights into the development of these characters: Mary Yukari Waters, Jonathan Penner, Larry Williams, Eleanor Inge-Baker, Liza Mattison, Catt Foy, Travis Megill, Leah Henderson, Veronica Castro, and Becky Erpf.

I've had the privilege of being influenced by a number of talented, passionate educators. Heartfelt thanks go out to each of them, especially Jay Bates—my ninth grade English teacher who struck a deal guaranteeing I'd pass the class as long as I kept turning in my crazy stories.

I thank my mother, Barbara Anderson, for handcrafting fabric-bound books for me to write in as a child. For passing along his dark sense of humor and wild imagination, I thank my father, Dee Anderson. For showing me the magic in the world through the eyes of a kind-hearted storyteller, I thank my grandfather, Vandis Hathaway. For constantly reminding me that writers are rock-stars too, I thank my dear friend and sister, Christina Anderson-Esau. For her support, kindness, and tireless efforts raising the amazing man who became my biggest fan, I thank my mother-in-law, Frances Gonzales.

Thank you to my cherished friends all over the map who have spent countless hours encouraging my dreams and fueling my imagination.

Special thanks to Spalding University's MFA in Writing program, and the life-long camaraderie flourishing within the prolific writing community they've established.

Permissions

Every effort has been made to contact copyright holders; in the event of an inadvertent omission or error, please notify the publisher.

Howitt, Mary. "The Spider and the Fly." *Sketches of Natural History.* New York: Johnson Reprint, 1970. 123-28. Print.

First publication: London: Effingham Wilson, 1834
Publication date note: *The New Year's Gift* (1829)

Forthcoming

Want to receive a FREE book?

Sign up at VGAnderson.com

More info can also be found at:

twitter.com/vandersonauthor
facebook.com/vgandersonauthor
instagram.com/gypsyauthor

To leave a Goodreads review, please visit
Goodreads.com and search for
The Light in the Sound by V. G. Anderson.

About the Author

V. G. Anderson was born in SLC, Utah but grew up in the Pacific Northwest near Seattle. She has degrees in Psychology, Journalism, and Creative Writing from Indiana University, and an MFA in Creative Writing from Spalding University, Louisville, KY. Her short fiction and poetry have appeared in US, UK, and Canadian literary magazines, and she was nominated for a Pushcart Prize in 2018. She's a full-time writer and freelance editor, currently exploring the US in a vintage "tiny house" RV she renovated with her husband, Josh. Learn more and follow her work at VGAnderson.com.